I0682253

SHADOW SELVES

SHADOW SELVES

A NOVEL

by

Daniel Hill Zafren

TIME TREASURES BOOKS
Books treasured for all time

Copyright © 2004 by Daniel Hill Zafren

Originally published by Beard Books
Republished 2006 by Time Treasures Books,
Charlotte, North Carolina

ISBN 13: 978-0-9778892-3-8
ISBN 10: 0-9778892-3-8

Printed in the United States of America

The cover image is Shadow, an oil on board painting by
New Mexico artist Dale Latta, and is used here with
the permission by and courtesy of the artist.
Shadow ©Dale E. Latta 2003
www.dalelatta.com

Cover design by John Cole, Graphic Designer,
Santa Fe, NM
www.johncolegrf.com

To those who dream

and

to those who dare to live their dreams

This learned I from the shadow of a tree
That to and fro did sway against a wall,
Our shadow selves, our influence, may fall
Where we ourselves can never be.

Anna E. Hamilton, 1843-1876

1

Whoosh went another wish. He was always wishing for some thing, wishing that he could be more than he was or at least different. When he was a boy he pronounced *wish* as *whoosh*, and that translated into this later reality. His greatest wish for the moment and for many moments was that he would not be so shy.

Snippets of his past came to him at unusual, unexpected times. Why he would all of a sudden remember this or that remained a complete mystery. Events or people from his earlier life would take on real substance in his mind, perhaps not as they really were but as he thought they had been. It mattered not because he relished such a power of recall. A further baffling aspect was that he could conjure up some of the minutest details of some memories while the features or peculiarities of others would totally elude him. Selective memory of sorts. But what forces were interacting in the selection process?

Here he was at the ripe-old age of twenty-three, just starting his first year at Blantyre Law School. It was the first lecture in the class on the Law of Contracts, and while Professor Dugan droned on about the possible ramifications of oral and written relationships between sellers and buyers, his hand stopped taking notes. All he could think of at the moment was Sheila.

He had not thought about Sheila for many years. He could not even remember her last name. She was the first girl he had a crush on. He was ten years old, and she had probably been about the

9

same age. They were in the same school and in the same class. She was bright, out-going, popular, and participated freely in all of the class work. He, on the other hand, was withdrawn, extremely self-conscious, and extraordinarily shy.

Sheila had short brown hair with bangs cut just above large brown eyes. A slightly turned-up nose at the tip, surrounded by a bevy of freckles. They never spoke, and she had never even acknowledged his existence. For all he knew she actually did not know he existed. Yet, that did not stay him from composing secret love notes and poems to her in his head and in a small notebook. It also never swayed him from his daily ritual of following her as she walked home from school. At a safe distance he would watch her slim frame as it gracefully moved down the sidewalk, his eyes riveted to the back of her calves as her skirt would sway from side to side. Often, she would have friends at her side, but this only accentuated his concentration on the distant object of his pulsating heart. At the end of that school year her family moved away, and he had his first experience in dealing with depredation.

Bryant Yorkwood did not really want to go to law school. Difficult times were brewing, and in 1964 Bryant's intelligent and politically astute father was convinced that a full-blown war was inevitable in Vietnam. His controlling opinion in the family was that it was vital for Bryant to be in school to get and keep a student deferment from the draft. If he had been asked, which he knew he would not be, he wanted to become a writer and had majored in journalism in undergraduate school. He had long since gotten over being totally withdrawn, but he remained unusually shy. Writing seemed to be a logical venture for one who is keenly sensitive as to how others might look upon him. Self-conscious was not what he wanted to be but there was no way to overcome it. Lost in a world of writing, he would not have to be involved in interpersonal relationships, there would be no pressure to make or sustain conversations, and no need for overt expectancies to be met. He knew that some day when he was considerably older and when experiences would have taken the sharp edge off of anticipation, he would then care less about the opinions of others. People would like him or not on his own terms. And, if they did not, such would be their problem and not his. But, that was then. This is now.

Bryant looked around the class, as the entire first year class had to take this required course. One hundred and forty three students, only five of whom were women. One hundred and forty three stories. He wished he knew them all so as to fill a book with them. How many were really here to become lawyers? How many were trying to escape from some form of outside commitment or some kind of conceived turmoil? The imagination of the writer being unlimited and unstoppable, reality was no match for that sort of enterprise.

Because women were scarce in the class, they had received great attention from their male classmates. Even from the first day of orientation and before the actual academic classes started, the more aggressive and eloquent men swarmed around the ladies. One young woman, particularly attractive, was the center of frenetic activity. That her name was Sheila was a symbolism that did not escape him.

Bryant had taken it all in from the sidelines. The competition was too fierce, too concentrated for his limited prowess. Not that he really minded it at all. He was here, even if not by total free will, and he was determined to do the best that he could to succeed. Yet, lurking behind this positive attitude was the negativism of his shyness. He had never related well to girls. He had few dates, and limited experience in amorous situations. He had never come close to a real sexual episode. This love-from-afar repose, initiated by the early situation with Sheila, carried forth to his contemporary life. The mystique of miscue.

There had been some brief encounters with romance. Linda, the girl he had met on a family summer vacation. They had kissed passionately, and he could almost still feel those soft full lips pressing against his own lips. Much to his amazement at the time, she had taken his hand and placed it over her breast through her blouse. He was frozen by inaction, but the episode stayed with him for years to come. The mystifying wonder of what might have happened if he had become aggressive. She had even taught him to slow dance, and the music of that era was so filled with passion that it fed his already romantic inclination. Songs of falling in love, young love and parental disapproval and negative influences, love destined to last forever, death and even suicide. The memory of holding her slim body in a tight embrace as they barely moved as they danced. The music twirling in his head. A yesterday of emotions. A world away. She lived in Florida. They had exchanged letters, but they soon became fewer and further apart until a cessation.

Then there was Doris. Her mother had died and she was taking care of her father and raising a younger brother. He had met her at a hootenany, the folk song fest at which Pete Seeger was the main attraction. Held every month, it was a meeting place for the liberal activist set, seeking kindred spirits in mind and song. Doris was studious and excessively serious, no doubt fostered by the great responsibilities she had foisted on her. Besides some pecks on the cheek, their romance was centered on long talks about many subjects. She talked and he listened. Bryant, the introvert, had always been an avid reader. Doris was also a bookworm. It was Bryant's introduction to the mutual worship of words, the romance of ideas. He knew from that experience that love needed to have a mental aspect as well as a physical one. Somehow, the contact with Doris grew less and less. She was always so absorbed in her role in the house, he felt that a part of him was suffocating. Another lesson to be learned. Any relationship will not grow without a strong participatory interest. To be together, a man and a woman must have a sense of togetherness. To share old experiences as well as new adventures.

There had been some dates, some minimal contacts with the opposite sex. Fuzzy faces, forgotten names. The wonder when and if he was going to find the life he would be comfortable with and excited about. There were plenty of stories by other males of their pursuits and conquests of females, and the writer in him usually affixed a certain fictional aura to the tales. Stories from the imagination can become tinged with reality the more often they are related.

As Professor Dugan droned on, Bryant's mind shifted to canvass his present posture. With his high academic record, he could have gone to any law school in the nation. The family was not rich by any evidentiary standards, but his father had saved enough money through frugal living to put his only son along any educational path chosen. Blantyre seemed to have much in its favor as a personal choice. It was one of the smaller law schools, yet it was attached to a large university. In fact, even the law school building was central to the Blantyre University campus. It had garnered a faculty of experienced practitioners, and it had a forward-looking philosophy by emphasizing the practical application of the law rather than the theoretical aspects. The entire university had captured faculty members not so much for their academic acumen or scholastic standing but for their experience in the commercial world. This unusual tact helped it to achieve a very high national reputation. The place to be today for preparation for tomorrow. Even though the law was not Bryant's utmost choice, this seemed to be the right place to be.

His thought processes would have carried him further on but the shuffle of the students towards the exit broke his reverie. Reinforcement came from the voice of Phil Montague, his next door neighbor in the dorm and who had been sitting next to him during the lecture. "I told you to sign up for the Law of Dreaming and not Contracts Law."

Phil Montague was also an only child, but he came from a prominent Philadelphia family. His father was a judge on the municipal court, and Phil's future was preordained. Overweight and constantly jolly, he was not what one would describe as a typical lawyer candidate. For Phil himself, he accepted this expected role knowing full well that he really had no other recourse.

It took only a few seconds for Bryant to respond to the witty remark. "Ah, but to dream well one must fall asleep readily. This has to be better identified as the Introduction to the Law of Dreaming class."

"A wise man. A quick discovery, but I can tell that you took few notes. I doubt if you can afford to reference mine."

"Then I will have to wing it as an offshoot of my Law of Flying class."

13

"That is like flying by the seat of your pants?"

"No, that is the Law of Pleating."

"Mercy! I give up. Let's go to the cafeteria for an early dinner."

As they walked towards the huge cafeteria that was shared by all of the students of the University, Bryant took note of the early autumn foliage. He loved this time of year. The air was crisp and clear, and noting the colors also piqued one's powers of observation. The trees turned earlier in New England. Even the waning September day had a noticeable chill to it. His writer's outlook searched for an analogy. The impending coolness hung over the university as a cape.

He turned slightly to Phil's direction. "I sure do wish that there was at least one elective course in the first year. These required courses, especially Common Law Pleading, are a bear to get through, and I suspect it is going to get worse the deeper we get into them."

"These are the ax courses. If you make it through the first year then the higher powers feel you have a chance of getting through the entire three years. Otherwise the business world beckons, my friend. To reach the elite position, much suffering has to be experienced. They all did it, and there is no chance they will relinquish the thought of you going through it any easier than they had it."

"Now that is a gruesome thought. Evil is perpetuated."

"A truism. Accepting it makes it easier."

"But not easier not to lose my appetite."

"I never have that problem."

The food in the cafeteria was not of the gourmet type or even presented in any appealing fashion. However, the portions were ample and there was a variety to choose from. Since his mother was an impulse cook, he had gotten used to accepting whatever was available. Being fussy was neither practical nor logical.

There were many coeds in the cafeteria. Bryant's eyes shifted around the massive room, and occasionally he would catch a glimpse of a girl looking back at him, or at least he thought she was doing that. He would quickly look away, and would not dare to glance back. That was an unpaved road, and it did not beckon him to travel down it. He might not find his way back. What was that old rhyme: *A risk to take, find a mistake.* Or did it go: *A risk not taken, a chance forsaken.*

2

Later that night, nestled in his single room in the dormitory, Bryant pulled out a folder containing some of his writings. Right on top was the short story he had written when he was sixteen. It had won first prize in a young writer's contest. The Royale typewriter that he won was a thrilling achievement. It still had a place of prominence among his possessions. He had gravitated to an electric typewriter, but on occasion he would pull out the old Royale to rekindle a thought ember, to revisit the flowing creativity of his past. He took hold of the story and read it as if it were for the first time.

The Decision

Passing the tranquil settings with precise mechanical fluidity, the commuter train sped towards the city. Roger Burnette was on that same train every working day, carrying him to a job that held no meaning. Its only benefit was as a temporary respite from a home life that he could no longer cope with. This gray morning he had no interest in the newspaper still folded neatly in his lap. Instead, he stared out the window of the train at the box-like houses that streaked across his vision. No longer could he avoid the amassing problems. It was time to make a decision.

He conjured up Ellen's face. The small mouth that parted as easily into a smile of utter joy as a smirk of contempt. The intense eyes, and the freckles which appeared on her cheeks at the slightest exposure to the sun. Their courtship had been an unusual one, and the attempt to combine two separate religions only brought internal strain and the disdain from both sets of families. Forced to withdraw from others, their exile did not bring contentment but only a growing restlessness. A shaky foundation upon which to build a marriage. It defied all apparent logic but their love had actually contributed to the destruction of their marriage.

He loved Ellen, and he had no doubt that she loved him. As such, there was a degree of individual satisfaction but the combined needs were left in a precarious state. The mutual support to ward off outside pressures was lacking. It slowly eroded confidence in the marriage and compelled them to withdraw even further unto themselves. By shutting out the world they sought to prevent further erosion. However, it only served to exacerbate their predicament. Instead of gaining a period of repose, an accelerated deterioration took place, leaving the entwinement uncertain and the framework weak.

Then they thought the baby would solve it all. They were prepared to accept the offspring not only with the love of producing their own flesh and blood, but also with the additional benefit of it as a source for a cure-all. How foolish they had been! Instead of giving them the basis for filling the void, it only restricted them further in the attainment of any solutions. The baby became yet another source of stress and strain, causing constant friction.

Her pleading words sounded dryly in his ears and wrenched his very soul. As he stood by the door waiting for his ride to the station, clutching the baby to her breast, Ellen's usually forceful voice was trembling, "Where do we go from here? What can we do, Roger? You must decide to do something before it is too late."

He had no specific answer for her demand. All that he could do was mutter some empty words that everything would be alright. It was no answer at all. The reassurance was as weak as the generality of the words.

He had never been a quitter, but this situation was growing more painful and problematical. The thought of suicide actually filtered into a corner of his mind. His insurance would not be payable if he took his own life. Money was only one form of security. He owed more to them out of life than that, even if he owed far less to himself.

He considered leaving Ellen and the baby. Surely they would be better off without his constant depressing presence. Partial harmony might be restored in such a situation. Perhaps in some sort of individual isolation he might find himself and recapture an incentive to move ahead. If it were not for the baby, this could well be a logical and reasonable solution. Yet, as parents they needed to stay together. Neither one of them believed that a child was better off from a broken home. Surface cohesion, in spite of itself, presents a degree of security and comfort.

There seemed to be only one acceptable alternative. It surprised him that he had not thought of it before. It might be a risky idea, one that might take great resolve and fortitude. If it failed, their misery would be even greater. Misfortune would be by their own design. If it succeeded they could build again, refreshed and renewed. It would not be easy, especially for Ellen. It called for sacrifice, drastic change. No set plan, no certainty, and no predictability.

Tonight, after the baby fell asleep, he would sit her down on the old leather sofa in the den and discuss it with her. The words formulated in his mind. "Ellen, you are so right. We cannot go on like this. We need an upheaval in our way of life and a drastic change in our future. This may sound totally illogical and ill-conceived but I feel that it might be the only way to turn things around. We must start over again. I will quit my job, which I hate anyway. We will move to a different part of the country. Just studying where to move and making a selection might be a cohesive influence. New routes for a fresh beginning. By discarding all practicality, confronting reason head-on and tempting fate, it just might work for us." The more he envisioned presenting this scenario, he actually felt himself getting excited about the prospects.

He could not relish this newfound sensation for very long. A piercing screech penetrated and obliterated his thought processes. Screams, flashes of light, and the sleek aluminum train was suddenly motionless. Tranquility had vanished in an instant. Weightless, a burning pressure settled in his chest. His body grew hot, very hot. His extremities turned icy. Time had stopped, and with it all things of consequence ceased. Ellen would never know his decision.

For a person of his human frailties, writing was both a savior and an elixir. As he stared at a copy of the student-written university newspaper, *The Blantyre Voice*, he thought he might try to get on the staff and write some articles. It was a thought that would recur over the ensuing days, a soothing thought that permeated his daily ritual of the study of the law. Engrossed in minutia with repetitive rules of the law, it was a wonder any person emerged from such a study with a modicum of reasonableness left.

Bryant was just not sure where all of this was taking him. Theoretical inclinations were difficult to adapt to. He could not give up the personal writing completely, even though the study of law was proving to be pervasive. Then there was the seething repulsion of the unjust war in Vietnam that the United States was getting immersed in. He did not know too much about the burgeoning hippie movement, but there was definitely some attraction for breaking away from the staid shackles of societal restrictions. Perhaps there is a connection between free love and free advice. They both feel and sound good for the moment but are filled with less significance in the after-event. Just when does a consequence enter into the equation and sway one from an original impulse to act? Maybe it was just his personal weakness of thinking too much before deciding what to do and how to do it. He thought about things so much that he was often so immersed in the thought trip that he lost sight of where he had started and where he wanted to wind up at. He doubted that he would ever change, and he was not sure he wanted to change. After all, it was not so bad to be known as a thinking person.

One must live the way one thinks or end up thinking the way one has lived.
Paul Bourget

3

By the next week, Bryant's resolve had congealed. After his daily classes, he entered the office of *The Blantyre Voice*, the student run weekly campus newspaper. He was convinced that he needed to balance his law studies with article writing about contemporary affairs through the eyes and thoughts of young people.

Instead of finding the editorial office teeming with activity and creative enterprises, the space was rather small and quiet. Seven desks cramped together, idle typewriters and a lone telephone on the desk by the one small window. One young woman was present at the desk furthest from the door. She was typing slowly at the machine before her, lost in her pursuit. As she glanced up over her glasses, it was almost as if she was resentful of the intrusion. "Are you lost?" Her voice was low but demanding.

"Constantly."

"Reassuring to know that I am not the only one." Her smile was warm and friendly. Perhaps she had welcomed the break from her task.

"If I were truly lost, is this the kind of place in which I might find myself?"

"Maybe. It would not be without some risk."

"Have you found yourself here?"

"I'm still looking. But, I have not yet given up."

21

Bryant moved closer to her, attracted not only by the facile conversation but also by her appearance. Short black hair fell straight below her ears with bangs nearly concealing her eyebrows. All accentuating coal black eyes atop a short pointed nose, the eyes not losing their piercing quality through the lenses of the glasses. Firm, well-formed lips pressed together over a narrow chin. Not what boys in their collective appraisals might call a "looker," yet there was something quite alluring and captivating about her. Maybe it was the composite picture, adorned by a thin frame with small breasts barely discernible through a white, high-necked blouse.

Her stare met his, and as she spoke her voice could easily be interpreted as either stern or light-hearted. "Undressing me with your eyes?"

The question sort of took him by surprise. Rather than stammer an instant retort, he delayed its utterance groping for a neutral response. "Never really tried that. Do you think it is possible?"

"It is just an expression, silly. It means you stareth too much. Anyway, even if you had such magical powers, I think you would be quite disappointed. I am far from a sex object."

"Ah, disappointment is in the eyes of the seer, not the focal point."

"All I see is that you are a master of words, perhaps even an intellectual worm that can wiggle out from any corner."

"Not really. I am just exercising my philosophy of personal non-arson. I try not to burn bridges behind me, so I am sure not going to burn any before me."

"Powerful wisdom for one so young."

"I suspect I am just the replica of what you yourself see in the mirror."

She broke out into a broad smile, straight white teeth radiated warmth. It was an endearing gesture. "Enough of this bantering. Why have you interrupted me?"

He was tempted to say what he was thinking at the moment — *Be my friend, I sense you are just the kind of person I can warm up to and relate to.* Rather, he said in a tone more timid than he wanted, "I was hoping to see someone about doing some writing for the paper."

"Hey, that's my tact! I am attempting to do just that, and I am doing a really poor job at it. But, I am just a lowling here. You need to talk to the editor, Mike Plaskowski. He will not be here until early this evening."

"How long have you been doing this?"

"Two hours."

"No, I mean writing for the paper."

"I started in my freshman year, two years ago. I write a regular column on the oppressed rights of those who are afforded few rights in this restricted society — Negroes, Indians, women, migrant workers, and the handicapped.......to name some examples."

"A fertile field to plow."

"I feel like a lone wind blowing over that fertile field. A presence with far too little impact."

"I have heard of instances when even a slight wind can fill the sails of a mighty vessel and can move it through troubled waters."

In a voice filled with drama and repose, she shouted loudly, "More wind! More sails!"

"A fervent crusader. How did you embark on such an undertaking?"

The momentary silence was deafening in its own way. It was apparently an inopportune question. He instinctively felt that he had crossed an invisible line.

"I am a cripple."

That was the sort of person that Rika Guastella had evolved into. The defect at birth that left her right leg deformed and weakened had given her compensatory strengths in other directions. Her intellect surged. She had graduated high school at the age of 16, and was now on the Dean's list in her third year at Blantyre. Quite outspoken and undaunted, she would not hide from the world or run away from her disability. Even in front of this boy who was paying her more attention than she was used to, she was not going to hold back any punches. Shock treatment based on her total candidness. It either brought out the worst or the best in people. The worst, which she had seen time and time again was to be treated with disdain or totally ignored as if she was not even a member of the human race. Secretly, she wished it would bring out the best in him.

Bryant then noticed for the first time the cane leaning against the wall by the girl's side. He studied the expressive face before him. It was important for him to say the right thing. He did not want to offend her, and he wanted to become better acquainted with her. She had already made an inroad into his shyness. He did not want to say something trite such as we are all crippled in one way or another. He did not want whatever he might utter to be interpreted as a form of pity. His voice was soft and yet earnest when he did finally speak. "If you hadn't told me, it would have been the last thing I would have noticed."

"Because my deformity is hidden by this desk?" Her voice was challenging him to respond.

"No. Because it is overwhelmed by all else I see and hear."

Inwardly, Rika knew that she was not going to be disappointed by this young man. Her entire life had been a struggle not so much to overcome the physical aspects of her disability but to bear the emotional scars. Ridiculed by schoolmates, scorned by the conventional social system, she had learned by default to make her own way, to need as little as possible from other people. That worked well to a point, but as she grew older, particularly here in college, a seething dependency arose. It was not for companionship. It was not for approval of the person she had become or what she may do. It was for a basic recognition that she was a human being and belonged to that grouping even though she was not perfect in human form and was considered and treated as an outcast. What hurt the most and what served as a constant reminder was that her brother and sister were physically complete but had gone on to abuse that totality by their distorted visions of their place in the scheme of life. It was baffling to her why people get to the point where they believe that things and accomplishments are owed to them and that they need not make any effort or contribution towards such an endeavor. It almost sounded as if she was feeling sorry for herself, but she was not. Let others waste their pity on her. She would do what she wanted, and always believe that life's favors were to be earned and not bestowed on her.

Rika stared at this boy who represented a sudden and new development in her course of action. If a male could be cute, he was that. Ruddy cheeks, glistening hazel eyes, and a full head of curly hair. She really could not tell if he was waiting for a response or merely enjoying a quiet moment. "You must come from a line of diplomats. That was a saving remark."

"Worse than that. I dabble in writing, but it was fact and not fiction that I spoke."

"Well, isn't that a coincidence. I fancy myself a writer and, thus, my role here writing for the paper. Yet, I am having the darndest time stringing the words together. I know in my heart that war is unjust, yet how do I say it without simply echoing the profusion of thoughts already spilling out from the anti-war movement?"

"While forcefulness can certainly come from originality, it can also come from repetition. Cull the important points and present them in a different format, such as an argument in court."

"I will need a lawyer for that."

"Would a law student do?"

"You aren't?"

"I am."

"If you are a stuffed shirt, how can you move fast enough to chase an ambulance?"

"You bribe the ambulance driver to slow down."

"Ah. You should not be so liberal in revealing the tricks of the trade."

"What are you majoring in?"

"Physical Ed, of course."

"A cynic too, I see."

"Just bridging the narrow gap between psycho and psychic. I am really studying to be a call girl."

"I think I am trying to bridge the gap between humility and futility."

25

"I am merely suspicious about why the interest in me. If you are here to write for the paper, you need to see the editor."

"Maybe you are psychic. That is why I came, but right now I find it much more engrossing talking to you."

"Why is that? Are you trying to find out if one is physically crippled then the mind must also be dwarfed?" She regretted saying that the instant it came out. "I am sorry. I am really not as bitter as that might sound, and I certainly did not want to put you in the category of the too many ignorant people who neither understand or are concerned about my kind of people."

"Apology accepted. You are very hard on yourself, I can see that. If you will let me lift myself up to your true level, I think I can be your friend. I would very much like to be your friend."

Rika was speechless. Such a warm, genuine social overture had never been made to her before. It took here completely by surprise. She had never been out on a date with a boy and had never had one even want to be her friend. She had few female friends, and the ones she had were short lived as soon as her deformity detracted from their so-called normal activities. She was at a loss on how to react and clueless as to a response.

Bryant was also at an impasse. He had already communicated for a longer period of time and with more earnestness than he had with any other girl. It surprised him and delighted him both at the same time. Her actual deformity was hidden by the desk, but the thought of it left him unperturbed. After all, he had his defect as well. Hers might be more apparent than his, but neither would detract from the other qualities of a friendship as a mean spirit or evil disposition might.

"A shadow friend?" she asked inquisitively.

" I may be sorry to ask this, but what is a shadow friend?"

"One who is with you when the sky is sunny but abandons you when clouds appear."

"Oh, a shallow shadow."

"It actually comes from an old saying by Benjamin Franklin.......*A false friend and a shadow attend only while the sun shines.*"

He extended his hand. "Before our friendship is sealed, and we see whether it can weather all weather, I should introduce myself. Bryant York at your service."

She firmly grasped his outstretched hand, and the slight touch of skin against skin felt reassuring. "Rika Guastella."

"That is an unusual name."

"My parents are Sicilian. I am named after my grandfather who died before I was born. His name was Enrico. Enrika is the female transition, and that is actually my full name, but I have always been called by the shortened Rika."

He had been this brazen, so he might as well push his luck. "Will you go out with me?"

"On a date?" Her voice was a bit higher than she wished.

"Yes."

"That was a short friendship."

"Friends can't date?"

"And stay friends?"

"It can happen."

"Maybe. But, why so pushy?"

"I have this gnawing feeling that I want to get to know you better. I think that would be best one-on-one, with no outside distractions."

"While we are still friends, I have a confession to make. I have never been out on a date. No boy has ever asked me out." She looked deep into those hazel eyes, waiting with great anticipation for his reaction.

Bryant shrugged his shoulders. "Their loss as I see it."

"Alright. I will accept only to find out what it is all about."

Rika was not sure where her thoughts were taking her. She did not sense pity in his invitation, and there was no apparent ill motive for him to be straddled on a date with the difficulties her physical attribute presented. There would have been easier ways for him to be sorry for her than to ask her out.

He smiled and moved closer to her. "Which dorm are you in?"

"I am a townie. My family's house is not too far from the campus. I will write my address and telephone number on this sheet of paper. You can call me if you change your mind."

"I am too excited to change my mind. I have no car, so if it is too far to walk I will pick you up in a taxi. Does Saturday night, 7:30, for dinner and long conversations sound agreeable?"

"It is a long walk, but you look like you can handle that. Do you like pizza?"

"Yes, very much."

"There is a wonderful pizzeria just around the block from my house, so you will save transportation expenses. I can make it that far. We can hobble over there together."

"I hope I won't slow you down. I am a deliberate walker."

"A deliberate fibber is more like it. Oh my, look at the time. My dad will be waiting for me outside. He picks me up as my personal driver."

"You have something special to tell him, I hope."

"If he will believe it. I often make up stories just to keep him amused, and he will probably think my imagination is in flight."

She stood up, bracing herself on the edge of the desk as she reached for the cane. She let him take a long look at her deformity. Her skirt, rather than hiding much of her distorted leg, only accentuated it next to her well formed left leg. An unsightly revelation might bring him to retract his offer. She searched his face for a grimace, scanning his bearing for any slight display of disappointment. Nothing she could detect, and she was good at reading the signs. Just a hint of a smile on the lips. Her smile echoed his and she was determined that her foundering would not detract from the promise of this moment.

Bryant stared at the door long after she had gone. A certain lightness spread over his being, and it had been a long time since he had felt this good about himself. Perhaps shyness is its own reward. It is a shield from the thrusts of disdain. It had allowed him to get close to her by opening himself up. A remarkable achievement for him.

He sat down and read her unfinished article still in the typewriter.

GLOOM 101

As war clouds form over our land, Blantyre is thrust into darkness. The gloom is a fog, covering up what might otherwise be seen clearly. If the young are truly to inherit the Earth, they must take action to make sure that the rights and principles we hold so dear are there to bask in. We must preserve them to make sure they are universally applied to all people, no matter what the color of their skin, the religion they practice, or their ability to fully participate in the feats of every day living. We, the young people, cannot sit back without protest for the course being set by others. If we are called upon to make sacrifices then we must have a say in the plan. We cannot blindly follow for we are bound to stumble and will be the ones who will have to deal with the ruins.

Bryant reread the paragraph. He then typed what he thought should come next. It would be up to Rika to accept that or reject it.

Therefore, as an introductory lesson, the young must first stop accepting without thought and without questioning what they are told and what they read. Not only is it their right to question what is presented, in these times it is a vital necessity to do so. It has ripened into a duty. If answers are forthcoming those should be judged for accuracy and sincerity. That calls for independent and objective judgment. Any position along the way can be a pitfall. We have all experienced twisted facts or an offering of only selected facts to bolster a desired conclusion. Then there is the bias to withhold

*contrary facts and opposing arguments. So, here are a
number of questions for you to ponder as an introductory
course for gloom so it does not turn into doom. If you
are not satisfied with the answers, investigate the
sources. A form of truth is out there. It may not be
absolute or even satisfactory, but not to try to find it
is the least satisfactory course of all.*

Is this a just war?

Are young people second class citizens?

*Are minorities, whether by classification or limitations,
third class citizens?*

*Why are the opinions of politicians any more valuable than
those of the people they represent?*

*Aren't the arms build-up, the threat of atomic weapons
and the amassing of great armies a threat to peace and an
invitation to the destruction of the world?*

*Why isn't there an interest and concentration in peaceful
change?*

Shouldn't democracy conform to responsibility?

*What should I do to make a safer, saner world for me and
my children?*

*This is not a comprehensive set of questions. Add any
questions you would like our elders to answer. Do not settle
for anything less than a complete and honest answer.*

He left the sheet of paper in the typewriter. He just knew that she would welcome it in the spirit in which he had offered it. As he closed the door behind him, a contact with the editor could wait. At this moment he had much to absorb.

> *An invasion of armies can be resisted, but not*
> *an idea whose time has come.*
>
> Victor Hugo

4

Salvatore Guastella leaned wearily against the car. The waning light made it obvious that the days were getting shorter. The leaves were turning color, and the crispness of the descending night led his mind to wander. Because of Rika's severely deformed right leg, she would never be able to drive herself anywhere. He and Jean had resigned themselves to do for her whatever she could not do for herself. Even though the family was anything but a normal family, they wanted her life to be as convenient and unrestricted as possible. It had not been easy for them to have a handicapped child after two normal ones, and the normal ones were not so normal after all.

Their son Bernie had been a restless spirit, and did not finish school. He had some minor scrapes with the law, and flitted from one construction job to another. He refused to live at home, but they had to pay part of his rent and even had to pay back rent several times to avoid having him thrown out into the street. He was not sure they were doing him a favor, but it tugged at Jean's heartstrings and it brought her some peace of mind. It was as if their son was in search of something, a thing that could not be identified. It left him wilted at such a young age, sapped of youthful enthusiasm and the prospect of a better tomorrow. Tess had not fared any better. She had become engaged at seventeen to a man they did not approve of but were helpless to convince her to see things more clearly. He was

32

a shifty fellow who broke her heart and spirit. It altered her perception of the adult world. She shunned all responsibility. She did not finish high school either, and rarely worked. She had withdrawn from the world and even constant nagging could rarely budge her out of the house.

Even though Rika made great demands on them physically and emotionally, she had always been a loving and delightful child. Her probing intellect and quick wit often made them feel somewhat inferior. Salvo had no doubt that in spite of the adversities she faced, she would be the one child who would become a success in life and one he could be proud of. Little wonder she had become his favorite child, and he constantly felt protective towards her.

Being a furniture salesman at a local department store had allowed him to stay close to home and to shoulder some of the burdens of care so that Jean could have some time to herself. Yet, she had never fully adjusted to the reality of having a handicapped child, as if it were her fault. She too was overly protective of Rika. They knew it was wrong, and even was stymieing Rika's ability to function on her own, but they could not seem to change. Their husband-wife relationship was weak, and there was no support, just the physical sharing of the burdens as they occurred. They clung to that as their life raft to preserve some cohesion for the family unit.

He watched intently as his daughter emerged from the building, her progress inhibited by her weakness. Yet, there was a dignity in her uneven pace, a pride in reaping the results of her efforts. For a keenly perceptive eye, Rika's use of the cane was more than just a crutch. It emphasized her presence and announced her chosen path. He marveled at her bearing. As she approached nearer he noticed the grin on her face in the twilight. That was a good omen.

He held the car door open for her, holding her book carrier until she was settled in. He closed the door firmly. After getting behind the steering wheel, he bent over and kissed her lightly on the cheek. "Why do I feel there is an announcement coming?"

She chuckled. "Remind me never to accuse you of not being clairvoyant."

"Even I can notice the obvious."

"Start the car, please. I am suddenly famished, and I know we are having mom's special lemon chicken for dinner."

"You are the one that is clairvoyant. How do you know what we are having for dinner?"

"Easy, Watson. A chicken in the icebox, lemons on the cutting board."

"Sherlock Holmes cannot hold a candle to you." After driving for a few minutes, he could not contain himself any more and blurted out, "Well, do I have to guess?"

"That might prove to be entertaining."

"O.K. You have been made editor of the paper?"

"No. Guess again."

"You have been told that you do not have to go to any more classes?"

"You sure are silly. One more guess, but a serious one this time. I will even give you a hint. Something has happened to me that you probably never thought would happen to me.......and me either."

"Now we are getting into tough territory. Let's see......you have made the football team?"

"And I thought you had no imagination not to mention a wild one at that. You leave me no other choice but to tell you since you would probably never guess it. I have been asked out on a date."

It left the elder Guastella completely speechless. As much as he may have wished it for her, he never dared to let himself think that such a wonderful ego-boosting event might happen to her.

She sensed the dilemma in his mannerism — to say something about it, to ask for details, or just to accept it without comment. She spared his decision-making. She volunteered all of the information in a swift torrent of words. "I was alone in the office. This boy came in, and I swear he had a halo over his head. I let him have it with both barrels, and he kept coming back for more. His responses to my barbs were tactful, completely gratifying. I have never encountered such an extensive and understanding sensitivity. Even after I flung at him that I was a cripple, there was no flinching, no adverse reaction in either words or action. He wanted to know more about me, to be my friend. It was then that he asked me out. It was like a script in a play. No, more natural than that. When I questioned him about his motives, he stated that he thought that would be a good way to know me better. Imagine that? With my disfigured leg and my boyish, sexless body, some guy wants to spend some time with me, just me. It doesn't even bother him about being seen in public with a freak."

The animation in her voice was refreshing to him. "You are not a freak, once and for all please do not say or think that. Your inner beauty is there for any one who takes the time and makes the effort to see it."

"Sounds just like something my father would say."

"I can't wait for your mother's reaction."

"I wonder if I should make her guess, too."

"That would be cruel. She will know something big has happened. When is this monumental event going to take place?"

"Saturday night, unless he changes his mind."

"And why would he do a crazy thing like that?"

"Because he might realize that the other fish in the sea swim better, are prettier, and more of an appealing catch."

"Poor fellow. The halo is fading already."

"Very funny." She poked him on the arm as they pulled into the driveway to their home.

As usual, Jean Guastella was waiting for them at the door. Her extreme protective nature long had overshadowed her own interests, and it bordered on a compulsion. Not that she was resentful but the gnawing feeling emerged strong from time to time that she had sacrificed her life for this child. She had given up the possibility of any personal quests to be the fixed homebody and primary caretaker for Rika who could not really fend for herself until she was in her early teens. Even then she was always there for her. What hurt the most in the few quiet, private moments that she had was the sacrifice of her secret passions. Jean was an emotional woman, deeply romantic in nature. She longed for the strong and loving embrace of a man, a man who would make her feel as the whole woman she was meant to be. All temptations were buried deep in her imagination, and when she dared to dream faceless men would make searing love to her in exotic and adventurous places. Salvo was a gentle, kind man, but he lacked the romantic spark she desired. He avoided intimacy. So, she sublimated that in the caretaking, the shepherding of Rika to and from school, accompanying her on as many mind-broadening activities she could think of. They went to museums, attended lectures, and any other feature inviting a mental discovery so that the outside world would not frighten her. Mysteriously, Jean became more afraid and timid as they went along. The expectancy of a regular life disappeared when she saw her baby with that badly mishapened leg dangling from her body. The composite of that wondrous child could not be completed. At that moment she resolved that her baby would be whole, be right in all other respects. While he never said anything about it, she had the sense that Salvo blamed her for this birth defect. Their closeness waned, and the marriage became superficial at best. Even the troubles with Bernie and Tess did not prompt unison of spirit and efforts. They were lost as to how to help, and too proud to seek outside help. They stumbled along doing their best for any given moment, knowing that they were just putting a bucket of water on potential big fires. What was emerging as her biggest problem was this belief that she had yet to start living her life. As this illusion grew stronger, her attention to other matters flickered. A woman had a right to love and be loved with passion. She yearned for such a colossal achievement. She wished no less for Rika. It loomed as an impossibility for them both.

Jean knew instantly that something was brewing. Both Rika and Salvo had broad grins on their faces. Even with the cane, there seemed to be a new bounce in Rika's gait. She bounded up the front steps in what must have been record time. After hugging her mother, her tone was markedly gleeful, "I have been seduced."

Jean's mouth fell open. She tried to speak, but nothing came out of her mouth.

Rika continued, especially amused by her mother's initial reaction, "Cajoled, preyed-upon, and seduced with ease, I might add."

Finding her voice at last, Jean asked in a feigned stern voice, "Have you been drinking?"

"Yes," Rika blurted out. "I have tasted the sweet nectar of life and I am totally intoxicated by it. I have been asked out on a date."

Once again, Jean could not speak.

The three headed into the house. Rika dropped her book carrier on the floor and made for the bathroom to wash up for dinner.

Jean pulled Salvo aside. "What is going on?"

"It is not for me to tell you. I think her greatest pleasure now is not over the fact of being asked out but in the telling of it."

At the table, the famous Guastella lemon chicken took on a new appeal, for Rika anyway. Ignoring Tess's cold and indifferent stare, she exclaimed with great animation. "I am starved. Being a desirable woman sure makes me hungry."

Impatience gaining the upper hand, Jean implored, "Is someone going to tell me what is going on here or do I have to start sewing a wedding dress and get my father's shotgun out of the closet?"

"Alright. Don't blow a gasket." Rika then retold the meeting of Bryant and the events as they unfolded.

At tale's end, Jean offered, "Oh, my. Prayers do get answered, even tiny ones. I can't wait to congratulate this young man for his taste in women."

The evening meal was more jovial than usual. Even Tess seemed bolstered by a new turn of events in an otherwise boring household. A thought in unison........*let Saturday come on angel's wings.*

Rika had great difficulty in falling asleep that night. She had no doubt shown Bryant her rough side. That was a real small part of her composite being. It arose as a defense mechanism. She needed to erect a tough exterior to ward off the personal indignities. A thoughtless and insensitive society held no forgiveness for people deemed to be a burden to the system. Her paramount soft side that she rarely revealed was her true essence. Had Bryant been perceptive enough to see that? He had now given himself the opportunity to discover it and to enjoy it. It was her opportunity also to open up to a person, perhaps more completely than she had ever done so before. It might prove to be refreshing even if the risk brought forth a fear of its own.

Bryant was also in a fitful sleep. Getting back to the dorm and burying himself in the casebooks, he was both proud and disappointed in himself. For a brief period of time he had overcome his shyness with girls. His thoughts seemed to easily bridge to speech. Yet, had he come on too strong? Did he overcompensate for his weakness by hurling himself at her? Had he been far too presumptuous to finish that article for her? Would she be disappointed in him when she would discover that he was a rather dull personality? It is said that the law is a jealous mistress. Shyness is a scorned lover. One could never fully predict where it might lead. He was not sure what he might do.....or not do.

He tried to calm his agitation by conjuring up a picture of her in his mind. The soft straight black hair. The gleaming coal black eyes. The full, child-like lips. A slim frame with an obvious flat chest. Not an image of physical allure or of raging desire. The more he thought of her, not once did the deformed leg rise in the panorama of her being. Had his shyness actually led him to this kind of maturity? Was he now serious minded? Had his perception become one of probing acumen? Rika was more than just a girl. She was the personification of his own sought-after character.

5

On the next day, when Bryant read the opinion by Benjamin Cardozo in his torts casebook, he was enticed into the glory of the law, led there by one of the giants of the law. He knew for sure that he had encountered his idol.

Right after classes for the day, he rushed off to the law library. He was on an absorbing mission. He felt a compelling need to read this jurist's words and to know as much about the man himself as he could find out. It was a most satisfying hunt.

Benjamin N. Cardozo was one of the most influential judges in the United States. Besides an intellect for the law, he had a literary gift. He skirted judicial jargon and promoted legal enlightenment. He was ethical, believing firmly that affairs be moral and right. Honest people could shape their conduct on the faith of his pronouncements. He believed that law is more than what is found in books, it is in the lives of people, in their conduct and behavior. He was a complicated and intriguing person, but his progressive judicial writings were influential and many persons from all walks of life respected him. He was an Associate Judge from 1914 to 1927 and Chief Judge from 1928 to 1932 of the New York Court of Appeals, the highest court in New York, and then became an Associate Justice of the United States Supreme Court from 1932 to1938. Two of his sayings lodged themselves in Bryant's mind as mottoes to live by.

39

Justice is not to be taken by storm. She is wooed by slow advances.

The great ideals of liberty and equality are preserved against the assaults of opportunism, the expediency of the passing hour, the erosion of small encroachments, the scorn and derision of those who have no patience with general principles.

After a couple of hours of reading the writings by and about the man, he understood how his influence could be so pervasive. He admired that kind of leadership, the common sense emerging from the people level and working its way up to find a place in the law. He vowed to be the same way.

Back in his room, the day's events had inspired him to turn back to his own writings. Writings of the past as his prelude to casting out influence in the future. From the folder, he pulled out a short story he had written a few years ago.

The Pain of Silence

Silence has its own characteristics. As a prelude to vocal activity it can be filled with tension and anxiety. As an aftermath of spoken words, it can be filled with the full range of emotional nuances from satisfaction to anger. Frustration or regret can arise from what was said or how it was phrased. The written word can be erased before anyone reads it. The spoken word cannot be taken back. The silence afterwards can speak volumes.

It was not easy for her to tell the man she had agreed at one time to marry that she was now in love with another man. Now that she had told him, in the silence that followed the torrent of words, she realized that she could have been much kinder about it. He was, after all, a sensitive and thoughtful man, and it was these comforting features that at one time made her think that she loved him. After nearly a year of courtship, this initial ease had been transformed into monotony. The sensitivity had become a symbol of weakness rather than strength. Drabness, indecision, and inaction dominated their moments together. So, when she met her new love, his vibrance and dynamic enjoyment of life swept her up in a ground swell of excitement that her own youthful spirit could not deny.

But why did she have to say such hurtful things in such a cruel manner? She had planned to keep her story simple and short, even offering her own weakness as the cause of her restlessness that led her to grab hold of temptation when it emerged so conveniently. Yet, the words did not come out that way. The good intent fell victim to her frustration with him. The words that ushered forth became a psychological analysis of his faults, with the inevitable conclusion that it was entirely his fault that he had lost her. She saw the pale blue eyes watering. The shoulders slumped perceptively. The taste of power was sweet upon her tongue, and she did not cease the outpouring of merciless condemnation until he was completely crushed. The pain was etched deep in the furrows of his brow. Even in the agony of the moment he did not attempt to defend himself. No surge for redemption. In hurt silence, he endured the verbal assault and then slowly walked away, leaving her in a quiet that weighed heavier upon her than any retaliation he could have made.

The silence was permeated with guilt. A dull throbbing in her head added to the stupor. She had hurt a person the way that she had always dreaded being hurt herself. If only he had been more forceful and could make and carry out decisions of his own. But he never did, never would. She could not tolerate a whole life of that. A poor excuse for the tactless barrage of words, accentuated by the now deafening silence.

She did not hear him enter the room. She looked up just in time to see him move towards her. His features revealed no expression of emotion, but she sensed that he was expecting her to speak. From the torn mental fragments, no words came to her lips. As he approached her, she became frozen with a terror that she had never experienced before. It blurred her vision of his uplifted hand. It accentuated the sound of flesh against flesh. A smoldering sensation rose in her cheek where he had slapped her so forcefully. She caught a fleeting look at his face before he turned and walked out of her life. The silence hurt as much as the cheek.

6

"Are you crazy? What are you trying to prove?" Phil's voice was filled with a cross between exasperation and condemnation. "There are lots of girls out there, those that are not straddled with a physical impediment."

Bryant looked at Phil regretting that he had told him about Rika. Sure Phil was entitled to his opinion, but just because he told him about the forthcoming date it did not give him an open invitation to meddle into something that was basically not his business. His choice of association was still his private matter. He had thought that by imparting this event to Phil it would be a way of sharing a friendship based on other than their law studies. He certainly did not expect to be greeted by this harsh reaction. Now, he had to explain himself or shut the door entirely. He opted for the explanation to also serve as a solidification of his own judgment.

Bryant swallowed. Perhaps if he approached it from a legal perspective a resonance of reason and understanding would surface. "There has been a big push in recent years for the protection and enforcement of civil rights. Yet, one disadvantaged group is flagrantly absent from coverage by any civil rights legislation, as if they have no rights that need to be protected. The disabled have been scorned, abused, not tolerated, and victimized in the workplace and in nearly every economic and social scene. Burdened not only by their afflic-

43

tions, those handicaps have been grossly exaggerated by a noncaring populace so that any physical or mental incapacity is wantonly affixed as a symptom of ineptness and incapacity by an insensitive, uninformed public. Not worthy of protection by the law is the apparent conclusion. Therefore, the handicapped have been forced to face societal restrictions and limitations. They are relegated to a role where they must tolerate unequal treatment. They have no political clout, no spokesman to carry their banner and to promote their cause. It is as if society is ashamed of them. They are modern day lepers. Rather than helping them to become the full productive members of society that most of them can be, they are put down and shut out from opportunity. They face physical and emotional barriers at every turn. Housing, education, transportation, public accommodations bear a discrimination to them no less evil than that based on race, color, ethnicity, or religion. It is totally unfair and highly prejudicial to deny these wonderful human beings their chance to gain a foothold in achieving their potential."

Phil shrugged his shoulders. "I did not mean for you to get on a soap box. Sure, they deserve some legal status. I can agree with that for them as a group. What I am merely trying to say, or even trying to convince you, is that with your sorrowful history of relationships with girls, it would be much simpler and even more enjoyable for you to cultivate a romance with a girl who suffers no restraints in giving you what you need."

"I am surprised and quite disappointed in you that you can even allude to a mistaken belief that just because people have some physical handicap that they cannot partake of all the pleasures that a man and woman might have together."

"Are you really sure of that? Frankly, I do not know as I have never tried to make love to a handicapped woman. I know you haven't, so how can you be so sure that they are normal in that department?"

"No, I do not know as a fully blown scientific fact, but I am sure not going to approach it with a negative. I feel that it is the same until some indication proves otherwise. Sure, some physical hardship might make it difficult or impossible, but some so-called normal people also have difficulties in that area whether self-imposed or by virtue of some outside influence."

"I am not going to argue with you. You speak in generalities. What I am just trying to convey to you is your situation as it relates to common sense. By your own admission to me repeatedly, you are socially handicapped. You therefore need a normal girl so that your own experiences are not further complicated."

"And what is a normal girl? It is, and always will be, an elusive concept. What makes people desirable or given a measure of human worth is the composite of their thinking, their feeling, their principles, their ideals, and their dreams. From such stuff the total person emerges. We all have blemishes of some kind. If not on our bodies, on our character. It is just that some are more obvious than others."

Phil could see that he was taking the wrong approach. "Sorry. I did not mean to bring on such a tirade. I just do not think the role of martyr suits you. I just do not see why it is necessary. To me, life already is far too complicated. Why take on additional difficulties if you do not have to? Then, you probably wind up at a point where you may know what you are doing but in the process you have long since forgotten why you are doing it."

Bryant felt himself calming down. Underlining the discussion was the knowledge that Phil meant well even though he has the same bias that so many others share. "Look, Phil, I appreciate you being concerned about me. I am a big boy now, and I like to think I know what I am doing. Even if it is not fully clear, I am the one who must meet and endure the consequences. In a way this is new to me. All I do know at this point is that I have met a girl I was able to open up to, and for me that is remarkable. I feel awfully good about it, and I feel good about her for being able to accomplish that awakening. Beyond that I will just take it as it comes along. I owe it to myself to probe further. I do not see it as a martyr role. I am searching for my place as a human being. If in the pursuit of my own journey I can bring happiness or caring to others, that will just sweeten my quest. We all deserve to find our niche in the total picture. That is, to me, where the sense of belonging is realized. I had grave doubts about becoming a lawyer. Now, just by an exposure to Cardozo's writings I think it might be a fit for me. One part, at least, for me as a person. At the same time, I need to explore the other parts. Love has always eluded me because I am so shy. I never gave it a chance even if the opportunity smacked me right in the face. Sure, I am not saying that this is love with this girl or even that it might lead to any romantic involvement. Yet, I do know that my shyness slipped into the background while I was talking to her. I also feel awfully good about her accepting to go out with me on a date. At the same time I think I was doing the same for her. A very human act, two-way. Not very complicated in a final analysis. In fact, rather simple. Two goods make a right." That clarified his thought process. Perhaps it was beneficial that Phil confronted the situation so openly.

Phil grew quiet, his mind adrift. Now that Bryant had spoken so calmly, it soothed his own agitation which had been buried beneath the surface. It was not all caused by Bryant's revelation. Because he was fat, many a girl had turned away from him. Being fat was, when he thought about it in such terms, a disability of its own. It prevented him from doing all he wanted to do, and it certainly made him be a person other than one he would like to be. He really had no basis to attack others who also fall outside of the perfect range. He tried to compensate for his obesity by being the constant jokester. His natural inclination was, however, more to the serious side. Instead of dissuading Bryant, he should be encouraging him. If there was a woman out there for Bryant, then there might be one for him, a woman who had Bryant's outlook, one who could bypass the obesity and appreciate him for the individual that he was.

The far-off look in Phil's eyes led Bryant to a silent repose. He knew well that there were moments when a person needed to be alone with his thoughts even if in a crowd at the moment. These insightful words of Jules Renard came to mind:

> *There are places and moments in which one is so*
> *completely alone that one sees the world entire.*

"I am off to study," Bryant offered with some urgency.

Phil nodded. "Study is good. Not good to understudy. Might wind up as an undertaker, not a lawyer."

Back in his room, Bryant stared out of the small window into the night. He thought of Rika, trying without success to tell himself not to count too much on this association. His romantic nature was overtaking any form of reasonableness. He envisioned holding her close, kissing those full lips. The wind howled, and he faintly heard her say, "I love you, Bryant. Bryant, my beloved." He closed his eyes, clutching on to the fading vision. He hoped that when he reached out for it again it would be there for real.

7

Rika sat at her dressing table looking at her image deep in the mirror. Compared to so many of the other girls at the university, she was plain, unappealing, and not at all feminine. She would not delude herself into thinking otherwise. There was no way she could change this rudimentary fact, and she frowned upon using makeup or even lipstick. Such adornments were not her style and totally contrary to her philosophy. People are who they are, and if they added artificial aspects to their exterior then their interior selves were bound to be artificial as well. She even shunned wearing earrings, and had never had her ears pierced. Bryant had met her in such a self-contained state. He had asked her out knowing that what he observed was all he was getting. She often thought that her lack of beauty was just another part of her faulty package. It was not as if she was sorry for herself. This was her life composite. She had learned to live with it and to make the best of it. It was what others had to deal with.

This was to be her first date ever. Sure, she was quite excited, and it was only an hour until he was due to arrive at the house. She had not spoken with Bryant since their meeting two days before. She had been thrilled to find his handiwork on the article she had started. Mike, as editor, thought it was a really good piece and suggested that the two names appear as the byline. The more Rika thought about it, she inclined to the posture that it would be really good if the two of them continued to do articles together. She would suggest it to Bryant at dinner. Whatever personal relationship would or would not develop, dual authors might well add a greater dimension to the scope of the articles. If nothing else, it would be fortifying to have another mind giving and clarifying ideas. For her as a perpetual loner, it might even be refreshing to engage in a joint effort.

Naked to the waist, she stared at her nearly non-existent breasts in the dressing table mirror. A small nipple emerging from just a hint of swelling of the flesh. As she placed a finger on a nipple, she confirmed that the sensations were right. It was an erotic zone, no doubt. She had heard that boys prefer big bosoms, and there was no need for her to fight them off, or ever will for that matter if such were the case. As she placed her small bra on the dressing table before her, even though she did not need one and rarely even wore it, she considered stuffing it with cotton. The thought passed quickly. It was inconsistent with the flight from artificiality and her dedicated desire to be as real a person as she could be. Bryant would have to deal with that on all fronts, chuckling at herself for the slight pun in her thoughts. Yet, it just was not fair. Theresa had an ample bosom just as her mother has, and a perfect body to go with it. As her sister, she had nothing. No hourglass shape, no shapely good leg, and no breasts. Even her eyeglasses seemed to pinch her face together. A deformed leg. Flat chested. Poor eyesight. Scrawny body. Not a formula for social success. Yet, she could not now say that she had never been asked out. Would she still have to say that she had never been kissed? And, would she ever know love? Could someone love this unappealing form? Could she, after harboring barriers of her own making to ward off hurt and disappointment, be able to love freely and completely? She had read about sexual acts of pleasure between men and women. Would she ever get to experience that area which loomed before her as a deep and dark mystery? Perhaps she was not ready for any of this. No, she was ready alright. In fact, she was overdue.

Theresa entered her room. The door had been slightly ajar. Rika did not cover herself. Theresa laughed softly. "You should have been a boy."

"Don't rub it in. If you really were a good sister, you would give me some of yours."

"If only I could." Theresa looked longingly towards the window and beyond. "None of it has done me any good. It only succeeded in attracting the wrong kind of men. And, after the conquest, it is basically useless. Now, I am all messed up. I can't keep or even get anything straight. Nothing holds any meaning. A good body for a woman is merely a distraction."

"You still wouldn't want to trade places with me, would you?"

"No. I have to live with who I am just as you do."

Rika turned around and looked Theresa directly in the eyes. "I have often thought you have the easier road. I have envied you for that. But, maybe it isn't all quite that way. I have learned one lesson repeatedly. The simplest effect or appearance can be distorted by so many underlying complications."

"I am not sure there is such a thing as an easy road. My road has reached a dead end. But, you are smart. I can't figure out the common things. I have no patience or tolerance with jobs or with people. My looks will fade, and I'll be left with nothing. You are going to make something of yourself. We will all be proud of you. Me especially, since I will know that for some it can be done."

If Rika had the ability to bound to her feet and rush across the room, she would have done so to embrace her sister. The instinct was stymied by her inadequacy.

Theresa turned and started out of the doorway. "Have a wonderful time with your beau. If he turns out to be really nice, see if he has a friend for me."

Just as Rika was finishing her dressing operation, her mother entered the room. Rika exclaimed, "It's like grand central station. Did you think I was going to hide?"

Jean came over and kissed her on the top of her head. "No. I just wanted to see if I could help you with anything. I am more nervous than you are."

"I doubt it. It may not show, but I am very nervous. It is a first date I should have had years ago, so I have many years riding on this."

"Yes, I know, my sweets. I pray it works out and is a happy time. Beyond its symbol, it is a natural occurrence. Now that the ice is broken, there will be other boys, other dates. I firmly believe that when you least expect it romance finds you. It is the doing with it once you have it that is often quite difficult."

"I hope I have that problem."

"Me, too, sweetheart."

"I just keep thinking how I will react if he turns out to be disappointed in me."

"And, what if he is disappointing to you? I am not biased, but you are a very special girl who needs someone who is also very special so that there will be a perfect fit."

"I have a feeling deep in my heart that he will not be a disappointment. It may be the very first time that my heart is overriding my mind, and I find that in itself exhilarating." She smiled broadly as she put her glasses on. She patted her hair to make sure there were no stray strands. "For whatever happens, I am ready."

"Your father is pacing in the living room. I may have to tie him down so that he does not follow you down to Luigi's."

"Better to tie Bryant down so that he does not run away." Her laugh came easily, and it helped to calm some of the bubbling anxiety. "You both will probably scare him away the moment he sees the rope."

She went down with her mother to the living room, and they all sat down waiting for Bryant's arrival. No one dared to speak. Jean kept rubbing her hands together. Salvo pretended to read the evening newspaper. Rika felt a dampness in the palms of her hands, and her lips were dry. At times, waiting can be most difficult.

Promptly at 7:30, the doorbell rang. Rika stood, grabbed her cane and went to the door. When she opened it, Bryant flashed a broad smile and extended his hand that was holding a single red rose. Rika returned the smile, taking the rose in her free hand. "It is beautiful. Thank you. Please come in. My parents are dying to meet you."

Bryant followed her into the living room. Mr. and Mrs. Guastella rose in unison, smiling. Salvo first shook Bryant's hand and then Jean grasped it warmly.

"Mom, could you please put this lovely flower in some water and put it in my room."

"Sure, dear. Bryant, please sit for a moment."

Bryant sat in an armed chair and said jovially, "I forget that in small towns a date with a girl is with the whole family."

Salvo offered with equal levity, "It is really an old Sicilian custom. We usually hold your wallet for security so that we are sure you will bring her back."

"It may be difficult for me to pay for dinner that way."

"I never thought of that. We'll just have to take your word for it. Where are you from?"

"New York City."

Jean had returned by then and interposed, "I understand you are a law student."

"Yes. I was not sure at first that the law was for me, but the more I get immersed in it the more I feel comfortable about it. I am glad that my father had pressed me to do it."

"Is your father a lawyer?"

"No, far from it. He is a high school history teacher. My mother is a secretary at the school. That is where they met, and still do their daily rituals together all of these years."

Rika, standing by the chair where Bryant was sitting, broke into the conversation. "See, now you know what it is like to be cross-examined. I think we should get started before they engage you in so much talk that you will forget that you came here to take me out."

"Not likely," Bryant asserted.

Jean rose with Bryant. "You can see who truly runs this house."

Rika responded thoughtfully, "I didn't know you realized that."

Jean smiled. "Bryant, please take good care of our baby."

"I certainly will do that. It has been very nice meeting you."

After handshakes, Bryant helped Rika on with her coat. She

smelled of soap, clean and invigorating. Five minutes in her presence and he was lost already.

For Rika, it was the first time a boy had helped her on with her coat. His hand brushed her arm, and a shiver went up her spine. A new kind of shiver. Not from a chill but from a thrill.

Once outside of the door, he moved to her left side so that her right hand would be free to use the cane. He held her arm as they went down the outside steps, one at a time.

On the sidewalk, it was already dark, and Rika turned to him and said gently, "You do not have to baby me."

"I want to hold on to you, to help you but also to make sure you do not escape."

She laughed. "Fat chance of that. You need not be concerned. I couldn't run away even if I wanted to, but I certainly don't even want to think of doing that."

It took about twenty minutes for them to reach the pizzeria around the block. Neither one noticed the passing of the time. Bryant held her arm protectively, and Rika enjoyed the support. It became clearer to her that there are acts of assistance that have additional dimensions. Firmly connected with an intention to convey more than help, it can bolster the ego as well as the body. Secretly, she wished that he would never let go.

The twenty minutes were filled with unceasing conversation. Each topic easily led to another, and both talked freely and with ease. What struck Bryant the most was that Rika was a keen listener. She held on to his words, and when a response was in order she did not just dive into it. Thought preceded words, and every subject was explored in depth.

Luigi's was a quaint, old-fashioned Italian restaurant with an obvious specialty of pizza. A small and quiet place, and they sat in a booth in the back as if it were set aside just for them. The waiting staff all knew Rika, and even Luigi himself emerged from the kitchen to kiss both of her cheeks. Bryant felt very relaxed in this near homey atmosphere. The pizza was delicious, and even though they sat there for over two hours nobody rushed them to finish and leave.

Their talking continued unabated. When Rika brought up the possibility of co-authorship of articles, Bryant was receptive to it. They decided to do a joint weekly article, tentatively called *Straight Arrow*. They held hands across the table, and by peering deep into each other's eyes all hesitation and inhibitions flitted away. The bird of caution and restraint flew gracefully from the nest. Rika could not remember when she had laughed and sighed so much. Bryant temporarily forgot what it was like to be shy, to be tentative. A transformation for them both by a joining of hearts and spirit.

As they left the restaurant, they kissed. An observer could not be sure who initiated it, but that did not matter. A mutuality had pervaded their beings, and a staid social inhibition was not a welcome intruder. A soft, lingering kiss. A warmth spread between them and through them. It was unrestrained by their coats, unretarded by the autumn chill of the night. A warmth that melted any lingering emotional obstacles either might have had.

After the kiss, Rika spoke first even though the embrace continued. Her voice was steadier than she thought it might be, richer than she recalled ever hearing it. "Whew. You really know how to capture a girl's heart. Now, even if I could escape, it would be the furthest thing from my mind. I am trapped by your character. Are all of the boys as captivating as you are?"

He looked deep into her eyes again, almost seeing his own reflection in the lenses of her glasses. That symbolism was not lost on him. "I beg to differ with you. It is you who have captivated me by your enchanting ways. I hope other boys are not like me as I do not want any competition for your affection."

She smiled and they kissed again. Reluctantly, they broke the embrace and started back to her house. They clung to each other, a manifestation of the wonderful feelings surrounding their being together. Neither was in a rush for the evening to end, neither wanting to relinquish any portion of the fresh, newly found emotion that cradled their souls.

Back at her door, they kissed again. She took off her glasses so they would not fog up or impede the kiss. The warmth of joining lips sealed their moment. "You are the first boy I ever kissed. Please pinch me. I must be dreaming, although it is a fantastic dream."

"I haven't kissed many girls, believe me, but I now know that they were not really kisses. A kiss is more than lips touching. The whole body and the mind participate in the act."

"I take your word for it. I just feel like I can go on and on just kissing you. A tear formed at the corner of her eye. "I had a wonderful time on my very first date."

"The first of many, I hope. I am usually not an impatient person, and this is not a way of rushing you, but I have never been with a girl that I feel this strongly about. I want to be with you as much as possible. Will you go steady with me?"

She chuckled. "My line of suitors is long, but I think I can swing it. Will you go steady with me?"

"If I can keep my heart steady. I do not want this marvelous feeling to end."

"Me neither."

They sealed their newfound commitment with another kiss. By comparing their class schedules, they worked out meeting in the cafeteria for an hour each day to be together and to work on their articles. Friday and Saturday nights were to be permanent dates.

Rika watched him go down the sidewalk towards the boulevard where he could walk to the University along a well lighted way. Even when he was out of sight, she lingered by the door. The taste of his lips was still on her mouth. The nectar seeping into her system was rich and sweet. The disbelief clouded the magic of the moment. How could a physically normal boy, a good-looking one at that, possibly have such tender feelings for a crippled plain Jane? It would undoubtedly be a question she would pose to herself many times. Perhaps it was something she should not question at all and merely accept the beauty of it. After all, there are some points on one's journey through life where being there is more important than trying to reason how one got there.

She opened the front door quietly, knowing full well that the family would be awaiting a report of the evening. They were in the living room pretending to be engrossed in a television show. Jean could not contain herself. "Well, must we beg?"

Rika looked at them intently. Even Theresa seemed to display an anxiety about the new element in their lives. "I had a marvelous time." She broke out into a broad smile. "He is wonderful........very wonderful."

"And?" her father interjected with a modicum of impatience.

"We talked. We ate. We laughed. I had my first kiss, and my second, my third and fourth. Each better than the one before."

Three smiling faces beamed at her. She could not resist the impulse. "We are getting married."

Three jaws dropped. "I am only kidding, but we are going steady. Imagine me, the wallflower of the century, going steady."

Later, as she lay in her bed for what she knew would be a sleepless night, her loins were aflame. She could feel her heart racing in her chest. The rose in the vase by her bed filled her nostrils with the scent of passion. She might not be a total person, but she was a complete woman. One of her natural idols was Helen Keller, and the sage words of that magnificent woman spilled into her mind. *What we have once enjoyed we can never lose. All that we love deeply becomes a part of us.* She was going to love Bryant better than any woman ever would.

Bryant also lay in his bed wide awake. He felt a fulfillment that he had not experienced before. He had overcome a life-long burden of shyness with a girl he had so naturally let into his life. He also had this strong urge to share with Rika all of his thoughts, all of his expectations, and all of his dreams. This was no small achievement for him. He basked in its glow.

8

On Monday, Bryant waited for Rika in the cafeteria as the noon hour approached. His heart was racing. Would the magic of Saturday night still be alive, or would the interlude have subdued its force and glow? Natural questions for a person who had doubted himself all of his life.

Rika took a deep breath before she entered the cafeteria. She was not sure whether she was dreaming, and a small unsureness tugged at her about Bryant being there. For all of the resilience she had built up over the years, she was face-to-face with her deep-seeded fragility. She could handle rejection by society-at-large, knowing that it was basically a cold, insensitive, and foreboding place. She could easily absorb the ridicule, the shunning by those she fundamentally did not care about. Now that she had met someone whom she had let her guard down with and let herself get close to, she would crumble if he were not here for her. With that indomitable reservoir of resolve exercised so consistently in her growing years, she entered the cavernous room. Ignoring the stares as she hobbled along, she saw him waving to her and her ego soared.

As if they were the only ones in that place, the embrace was long and intimate. The kiss a reassuring reminder of their newfound discoveries. Let all of the onlookers guess and pine away for what they may not have. Let them wonder for they see only a kiss and not

57

the flowering meadow in the young couple's landscape of life.

He helped her off with the bulky coat and they sat next to each other. Hands were clasped in celebration of the joining. "Can I get you some lunch?"

"No, thanks" she responded softly, "My mother always packs a sandwich and a piece of fruit. I will always be her little girl. Go ahead and get something for yourself."

"I am too full of emotion to eat."

"Not very sensible for a budding lawyer. Not good for me as I may need to lean on whatever strength you have."

"That kind of strength does not come from food, and whatever I have is yours to tap into. I was not sure you would show up. Saturday seemed like a long time ago."

"And I was not sure you would be here."

A mutual squeeze of fingers. A penetrating gaze into eyes and into the spirit. Reassurance that neither had to doubt the other. A lesson to hold onto. The moment was for them.

Rummaging through her book pack, she removed the sandwich. "Please share this with me. It would mean a lot to me. I am a great one for symbolism. This is my mother's wonderful meatloaf. A slice between two pieces of pumpernickel bread, and already cut in half. Maybe she is psychic. "

"Symbolism is important to me as well. How can I possibly refuse such a kind offer?"

"I hope that philosophy carries further than meatloaf."

"It does. It will."

"Good. I have not slept well since Saturday. My life has taken a very abrupt turn, for the best I might add, but it is going to take some getting used to."

"I have not slept well either. I think as we adjust to each other everything will fall into place. The uniqueness of a relationship like this is that it is to a large extent self-contained. I am no expert, but I think we have the ultimate control of who we are, what we have, and what we do with it."

She smiled as she gently pushed her glasses further up on her nose. "I will give due attention to all of the adjustments and channel all expectations selfishly."

"Sounds like a wonderful plan to me. I am with you all the way."

She caressed the back of his hand. "Not really knowing it, I have been waiting for you all of my life."

"And if you only knew what I was before I met you, you would see that my life has now just begun. I was so shy with girls. I could barely talk. A problem that I can now see was just a prelude to my self-discovery through you."

"I am flattered, kind sir, but I cannot take any credit for your flourishing. I am just completely bewildered that after one date we have done so much for one another. If I wasn't living it, I would seriously question its reality."

"The transformation is another sort of symbolism."

"A symbol with reverberating cymbals."

"An overture to our own symbolic symphony."

The collaboration for the next article then began in earnest. The very concept of symbols launched the endeavor. By Thursday, it was finished. Both very satisfied with its tone and tenure. One of the discoveries they made about themselves, and another common thread holding the fabric of their relationship together. They were both emerging activists. They had even found a fitting banner line beneath their column name.

STRAIGHT ARROW

Ex Umbris et Imaginibus in Veritaten!
(From Shadows and Symbols into the Truth)
Cardinal Newman, Epitaph at Edgbaston

by

Rika Guastella and Bryant York

The assassination of President Kennedy last year has left a deep wound in this nation. It serves as a symbol for the festering ills that gnaw at our society, particularly at the young. If we look around, there are many signs of the open wounds. The recent eruption between the students and administration at the University of California at Berkeley when all political activity not directly concerned with campus affairs was prohibited. To assert a force for freedom of speech, various segments of the academic and local communities adopted a tactic developed in the southern civil rights movement. A massive sit-in took place and some 800 people were arrested. This kind of protest is very effective. As a symbol, it stands for the power and stature of young people. It declares unmistakably that university students are the center of this generation and makes it known clearly that we look uncomfortably on the world we inherit. Such can be a driving force and a persuasive influence at both the local and national levels.

The symbols of the growing awareness and restlessness of young people are graphically presented by the hippie movement which is spreading quickly beyond its San Francisco origins. Young people are turning their backs to the elder society dictated mannerisms and teachings. They want to be who they are and not as others want them to be. This is reflected in their choice of clothes as they cast aside much of the so-called acceptable standards. They practice peace through love and a toleration of the Earth and themselves.

The music we all enjoy is also filled with symbolism. It is cause for reflection about who we are, what we are doing, and the dire consequences that may lurk behind unreasonable actions. One need only listen to Bob Dylan's prophetic lyrics, such as "The answer is blowin' in the wind" and "The Times They are a Changin'." Then there is Pete Seeger's "Where Have All the Flowers Gone?" Also, songs by Peter, Paul, and Mary and the Kingston Trio.

The Port Huron Statement issued by the Students for a Democratic Society two years ago has characterized American society as undemocratic and militaristic. These are our peers speaking their minds. It portends poor choices for national and international action by those in charge and serves as a rallying cry for all of us to ask the pointed questions, to seek other answers if the ones we receive are unsatisfactory, and to hold our leaders accountable for their decisions. After all, those decisions impact on all of us. They think that we have no clout because we are not part of the economic or political force. But, they are wrong. All of these movements, even if seemingly experimental, have already proven to be highly cohesive. College students across the land will no longer be silenced. If there is a full blown war in Vietnam, which looks like a distinct possibility from this view point, we must know that war is not historical destiny but just a human decision. Those who make those decisions must listen to those who will be called on to fight such a war.

The United States is the greatest nation on the planet. Yet, there are people and conditions here that urgently need to be addressed. Those groups that are exiled from the mainstream of American life, Negroes, the handicapped, women, as examples, will be the topics of future articles here in Straight Arrow. Becoming a full member of American society means that we must be aware of, and participate in, the changes that will bring an end to inequality and injustice. To be a rightful participant in our declared democracy we need to be constantly aware, consistently motivated for the pursuit of truth and peace, and to oppose any and all unreasonable actions.

It is time to take a stand. Watch, listen, question, and be on guard for yourselves and your peers. Our only persuasive voice will be in unison.

They were satisfied with the finished product, and gladdened that working on it together made it more productive and pleasurable. It fortified the resolve to work as a team and their desire to be together.

The article ran in the paper, and the campus response was heartening. The University administration, even if it did not endorse the pronouncements, could not criticize them. Blantyre, as an institution, prided itself as promoting and advancing free speech. A newspaper article was not going to daunt that perspective.

9

Bryant wrote to his parents about Rika. He had an open, honest relationship with his parents since childhood, and he was not going to hold back now. Since both had been in the New York City school system for a long time, there was little that they had not seen, little that they did not intellectually and emotionally accept as part of living in a societal community. Their reaction was as he had expected. They were happy for him that he had found female companionship and that he had overcome his shyness with girls. They cautioned him not to let it interfere with his studies, and they urged him not to let any feeling of pity or compassion color his true reactions. They were proud of him for the articles, as he sent copies to them. There would be much to discuss when Bryant would come home for the Thanksgiving break.

The words from Carlton and Frieda York were more tentative than Bryant interpreted them to be. The Yorks loved their only son dearly, perhaps too much if there is such a psychological manifestation. Secretly, they had thought his shyness was a good protective mechanism. They had seen too many youngsters fall prey to the influence of stronger personalities or to attractive causes. They knew all of this first-hand. After all, they had been liberals all of their lives and had gone overboard for causes they felt were just and long overdue. They had campaigned for Henry Wallace for President on the

American Labor Party ticket. They took to the streets to picket for clemency for the Rosenbergs when they were given the death penalty for treason, and even took unpopular positions in the school to thwart what they felt were unwarranted restrictions on the students and teachers. Unpopular causes reduce the circle of people who admire or tolerate the choices made. They had few friends, and the family corpus became even more crucial for their sustaining embodiment. When they first met at the school twenty-eight years ago, an instant attraction was bolstered by a background of independent thought and considered judgment. Both were well read and highly intelligent. Their taste in music, drama, art, and leaders ran in tandem. Deep down they knew this background would rub off on Bryant but they would not have been disappointed if it had only emerged in a dimmer light or in a more distant fashion. Knowing how activism is met by corporate America, they did not want any of his vast potential to be restricted. Yet, they nourished his probing mind knowing full well that they might not be able to control its outer reach. It raised a perplexing question. How to balance wishing your child be like you but also be his own person?

One evening as they sat together on the sofa in the living room of their apartment, Carl put his arm around Frieda's shoulder. "How many times have we seen it at the school? You can counsel until you are blue in the face but more often than not they learn the important lessons only through making their own mistakes."

Frieda placed her hand on his knee and gazed upon his face. It was a tired face, showing the many years of stress and adversity. "Yes, but that does not stop us from wishing it otherwise, especially with our own son. There hasn't been a day that I have not worried about him. Being an intellect and shy is a dangerous combination. I fear he will suffer much hurt and disappointment. Instead of concentrating on intellectual endeavors when he was young, I think we should have concentrated more on social experiences. Now that he is out on his own, I dread that reality and his perception of it may be two different things. I am not at all sure how we should handle this."

Carl looked deep into those brown eyes, seeing in an instant all of the years of their companionship and shared exposure to youngsters groping their way in life. They were pretty good at predicting how each would turn out. Occasionally, there was a surprise or two, but on the whole the future became the foreseen outcome. Yet, with their own son they could barely see past today. His love for his wife had mellowed over the years. There was familiar comfort in their unison but it was accompanied by a haunting dullness. Bryant's newfound event could well upset the fixed feelings and notions. For all of his professed progressive views and as an outspoken advocate for change in the societal fabric, he was most content with the status quo. So many times he had criticized others for what he was in truth himself. To project one image to others but actually being different to oneself. In the final analysis which is the real person—what he thinks he is or what he wants others to think he is? A daunting cynic, a flagrant hypocrite. Certainly not proud of himself, and to prolong confronting himself he also distanced himself from Frieda. She had always been a good wife and a person he respected for her ability to calmly handle difficult moments. She was an outstanding mother, and there was plenty of justification for Bryant to turn to her paced and rational reactions to events and people. When all was said and done, he was a virtual outsider to his own family. An outsider by his own choice, the chilling thought struck him.

Frieda recognized that far off expression and she had learned from many past experiences that it was best to let his inner debate come to terms with his temperament. Carl was burned out. Being a teacher for so many years can do that, and its lasting effects permeated throughout the family. She had once considered herself a vivacious person, but she had withdrawn so as not to make any waves to rock the only boat she knew she might ever have. She was sure that Bryant's shyness was a spillover caused by her inadequacies. The love for her son grew deeper as the outlet for her personality became more limited. She was glad she had prevailed on having him attend an out-of-town law school. He needed to be on his own, and to find his own voice. Her sheltering of him was smothering them both. He needed other role models so that he would not just emulate his father's views. Most women might be content to have what she had. After all, she had a job with challenging administrative functions, a job that also allowed her to take entire summers off. Albeit strained at times, there was a close family relationship. She enjoyed robust health, relied continuously on her quick mind, and could easily languish in a vivid imagination. That imagination carried her to places she would never see, to commune with the stimulating people she could not get close to, and to relish the exploits of her son, the lawyer.

Carl finally turned to her. "It is going to be an interesting Thanksgiving. I suspect that Bryant will have much more to tell us and will solicit little or no advice."

Frieda smiled and stroked his sweater-covered arm. "I think the days for giving advice have long since passed. Now it is for us to see what sort of fruit the tree has produced."

"I know we have talked about this many times before but one of the greatest failures of the educational system is that it does not prepare us to be parents, one of life's most important roles. Our parents, as immigrants, were so involved in adapting to a new country and surviving in a new culture, there was little time for anything but the basics. Now, as people are comparatively liberated, especially with the aid of technological improvements, and can turn their attention in greater proportion to developing the persons they bring to this life, you would think it would be an easy thing to do. Yet, when all is said and done, it is all guesswork and sheer luck in parenting. I think back on that time that Bryant almost joined that street gang, and I shiver. I think back when his best friend Saul committed suicide, and I am not sure if Bryant ever really did hear all of the words we spoke to him about that. He is now a man. I am not sure I communicated effectively with him when he was a child. How can I speak to him as a man?"

Frieda waited until she was sure he was finished with his thoughts. "It is the natural progression of life. From child to a man, he is still your son. That bond remains and I believe is even stronger as the level of treatment and respect becomes equal. He is a part of us. The family element in him and in us will make it easier to say and accept what is said. He will always understand our motives, even if the words don't always come out the right way. He is also astute enough to know that he will be a parent one day himself. That learning is a composite of practices and knowledge that comes from generation to generation, and I am not sure a textbook could ever capture the full range of its complexity. We have been good role models. We should be proud of that. As long as he opens up to us, and as long as he knows that we have his best interests at heart, it will be fine. You will see. The love will be reassuring to us all."

"I hope so. I am feeling my age, and starting to feel sorry for myself. Rather, I should feel sorry for you. I have not been the best of husbands."

"Nonsense. You have always been here. You are a good man, and I love you."

"I love you too, Frieda. I have not told you that often enough. You have been the pillar of my life. I am truly sorry for what may have been lacking in me for you."

"I am not sorry," she lied. It would be an act of pure cruelty to do otherwise.

10

"So, you're now the transformation kid," Phil pronounced after listening to Bryant's recitation of what had transpired with Rika.

"Sounds like a pretty apt description. I still have trouble believing it."

They were on their way to their class on Real Property. There was a distinct chill in the air, a prelude to the winter ahead. Most of the leaves had already fallen from the trees, and they swirled around on the expansive grassy areas where the wind was unimpeded. Too cool for a transformation kid cape, even if he had one.

"By the way," Phil looked sideways at him, "I liked the article. With so much going on, I wonder if we'll be able to finish this undertaking. Colleges truly are unique places. In one way they are a world unto themselves. In another way they seem to be in a very difficult position. The target of so many outside influences and looked to by others as the real prime mover. If full war prevails and conservatism predominates, law school may get swept away in the tide."

"You seem awfully pessimistic this morning. We can't go on with blinders on our eyes. Whatever role we wind up playing, we and our nation will be better off because of it. Until one convinces me otherwise, I go with that premise. It is our very own destiny that we need to get and keep control over."

"Easy for you to say. You expect only for yourself what you

want to do, what you want to be. For me, my father has a preformed mold that I must squeeze into come hell or high water."

"Have you tried talking to him about some possible alternatives? Surely he is a rational man."

"There are no such things as discussions. In his eyes I am not his son, a different person. I am him. He may be a judge and espouse all kinds of rational thinking from the bench, but he is adamant about me and my future. The pity of it is that I give in to him, and I can see that in these years they are all for him. There isn't even a crumb for me."

Bryant searched for the right response. "You are learning as you grow. That brings a personal strength, and you will know the time when it is ripe for you to stand up and make your own course. Perhaps the law will prove for you as it has now for me as a way of making a personal future. When you become a lawyer you will be more his equal. The crumbs are there. You just need persistence and vision to see them and to pick them up."

"You must be taking wisdom pills. Not nice for you not to share them with me."

"Not wisdom but merely a clear view ahead of me. The fog is behind me, and my wandering is over. A taste of what I might be able to do, and a wonderful girl to do it for and with. A formula that produces a will to make it all happen. If it will help you, I will be glad to report on all of my sightings along the way."

"I suppose my saving grace is that I am a tough nut to crack."

"All the more to keep trying. Work on meeting a girl of your own, just as you once encouraged me to do. Having a female to adore takes much of the sting out of life, believe me."

"A door through which to adore."

"Perhaps. Just open it and you may find out."

"Does Rika have a sister?"

"Actually, she does. And a very pretty one I might add."

"Doomed again."

"What happened to the door?"

"Who wants a fat slob to love?"

"Rika asked me who wants to love a cripple? Love comes in many shapes and sizes. Give it a chance. You too can become a transformation kid."

The Law classes became engrossing and enchanting times for Bryant. Attitude can be such a controlling force. With the image of Cardozo looming above it all, he grasped the concept that the law was not rules. He was being trained to think like a lawyer. To carefully gather and evaluate the facts, to ferret out all of the possible theories and alternatives, and then to determine the applicable law to each. If the fit was not precise, all the more challenging. If it was groundbreaking, what is called in the law a case of first impression, to go forward with determination to make new law. Lurking in the back of his mind was that for him there would be causes to battle for, maybe even unpopular causes.

That night, to placate his seething need for creative release, he wrote a short story.

Time as Thief

A clock has great significance in the rituals of everyday life. So many actions and activities are measured in terms of time. Yet, its symbolism is even greater. It represents a constant reminder that our lives are limited and that it is important that we give as much meaning as possible to all of the passing minutes.

He had never thought of time in those terms before. Like so many others, he just let the hours slip by, as they will, not trying to channel their passage constructively. Two significant events reoriented his being. First, coming across two old, wise sayings and a poem about time.

"No hand can make the clock strike for me the hours that are passed." Byron

"Lost yesterday, somewhere between

Sunrise and Sunset, two golden hours,
each set with sixty diamond minutes.
No reward is offered, for they are gone
forever." Horace Mann

The clock of life is wound but once
　　And no man has the power
To tell just when the hands will stop
　　At late or early hour.

Now is the only time you own
　　Live, love, toil with a will
Place no faith in tomorrow
The hands may then be still
　　"Now", by George H. Chandler

　　The second, was the call from the hospital that Melanie was dying and wanted to see him.
　　Melanie was a childhood friend back in the old neighborhood in Brooklyn. Their parents had been friends, so it was natural that they played together. They were the same age and went to the same school, good old P.S. 99. She was much more serious minded than he was, and under her influence their games often turned to a matching of thoughts and wit rather than with toys. She had even convinced him that he need not join the street gang, The Rebels, to be accepted, that there were those who would see him for his own person and appreciate him for that rather than for any group he might be associated with. In high school, they drifted apart to some extent, and it was the family bonds that kept

the relationship in existence. She then went off to college, and he took a messenger job with an insurance company. He worked up to a management position, and after marrying Corrine they moved out on Long Island to have and raise a family. Melanie came to the wedding with her parents, and she kissed his cheek and whispered in his ear that happiness could always be his as long as he had the courage to grab it and hold on to it. Those words stuck with him over the years. His family went to her wedding three years later and he repeated to her just what she had said to him. Her knowing smile was reminiscent of many a game they had played years earlier. There were social visits, becoming fewer and fewer as the years passed. Having a family with three children while Melanie could not bear children served to make the breach wider. Melanie's eventual divorce, and moving back to the old neighborhood to be with her parents only brought a momentary twinge of sympathy to his daily ritual.

As he entered the hospital, he wondered how many years that it had been since he had last seen her. Probably eight or nine years, swallowed up in the rush of trying to do acceptably whatever was demanded of him at a given moment. Not a good design to live by, but comfortable in its lack of having to plan and to be fully responsible for weaknesses. She was in intensive care, and her parents were huddled together outside the room, clutching at each other's now frail frames. They had

71

aged so much since he had last seen them. Nice people who had always had a kind and encouraging word for him. Time again a factor, as it was time for him to repay the favors. He clasped his arms around them, struggling to find the right words. "Thank you for calling me. I am late for her and late for you. I am so sorry."

A massive, inoperable blood clot, and Melanie's clock was ticking her final hours. As he watched her sleeping form in the bed, it dawned on him that it was ticking away for him too. Wires connected to machines revealed her vital signs, but the very essence of her feelings and thoughts could not be captured. Her eyelids fluttered and as she gazed up at him, a weak smile formed on her lips. She motioned him closer, and as he bent down to her lips, she uttered with the last gasp of her life, "Live your time for me too, dearest friend."

As he walked out of the hospital, he could not prevent the tears from flowing from his eyes. He had wasted time by wasting the friendship he should have enjoyed. Too late the agony for what had been unnecessarily ignored.

11

On Friday night they went to see the movie everyone was talking about — *Dr. Strangelove or: How I Learned to Stop Worrying and Love the Bomb.* Destined to be a classic in the film world, it delved into the absurdity of nuclear weapons and satirized the nonsensical strategy of *Mutual Assured Destruction* prevalent as the Cold War entrenched itself in the world scene. It graphically portrayed the dangers so apparent in the extensive technology of weapon building and the moral bankruptcy of military leaders. Lessons to be taken to heart.

Mr. Guastella had lent the car to Bryant for the evening's outing. After the movie, Bryant and Rika walked slowly to where the car was parked, hand firmly pressed within hand. The chill of the autumn night was no match for soul-generated warmth. Alternating between talk and silence, each moment carried a significance of its own. Since neither had experienced such a human closeness, each sensation arising from an action or a reaction was exciting. Their thoughts and emotions were not cast in the role of a first love but as an only love.

Before they drove off, the destination being the *Hot Shoppe* for pie and coffee, Rika turned to him and smiled that cunning way she would do before making an endearing announcement. "This short time has been so meaningful for me. It is so rewarding to love and be

73

loved. I had no idea of what I have been missing. What further amazes me is that in this brief time you have also become the closest and dearest friend I have ever had. The concept of friend and lover just seemed to be separate ones, and I now know that it is the combination that makes it so very special. A kiss from a friend and a lover is a double-decker. Mighty powerful stuff."

"Let's just confirm that theory here and now."

They kissed and its rapture was not disappointing. It spoke to them, directed them, and sent them to delight's door. The powerful representation knowing that in their own separate way they had been lost and that in the finding of each other they had each found themselves. Life's picture had turned to warm hues, fulfilling plans ushered into their explorative byways, and goals emerged filled with purpose and commitment. No small accomplishment, and there was an extra special pride in the achievement. In this small slice of time they had done for each what they might never have been able to do alone. The discovery and implementation of a purpose is magical by any standard. The impact did not elude them. It had even greater import at this moment, buried in a tender grasp.

The *Hot Shoppe*, a popular eatery for couples of all ages, was crowded. They waited twenty minutes for a table but there was no time wasted for them as long as they were together. Holding hands, their discussion centered on the impact of the movie and they agreed it would be a good lead-in for a future article. As they knew from the first joint article, their anti-war sentiment was equally strong. The intent was to do the next article on the handicapped with Rika taking the lead in its writing. She had written on the subject before, but it was time again to emphasize its importance. Ardent advocacy was desperately needed. Awareness is the vital first stage. Another march for rights to be led by the young.

Back at the house, after some polite conversation with the Guastellas, Rika led Bryant down to the finished basement where they would not be disturbed. On the sofa, the kisses became passionate. He caressed every portion of her body, even her deformed leg, through her clothing. She sensed his sexual arousal, and was in a sort of stupor of her own. She placed his hand on her nearly nonexistent left breast, and stroked his manhood through his slacks.

In a soft whisper she stammered, "I am sorry I am not more of a woman for you."

"You don't hear me complaining, do you? You are all I want, all I need."

"I know you excite me."

"I certainly hope so. This would not be good if it was strictly one way."

"I have never made love before."

"Me neither."

"I want to with you."

"Me too. Not as an act of sex. I want to show you that I love you."

"Will my deformity bother you?"

"What deformity?"

She giggled. "Good answer. A very good answer. Please undress me."

With the care emanating from a mixture of adventure and inexperience, with shaking fingers he removed each piece of her clothing until she was naked before him. It was more similar to another boy's body that he might see in the shower room than a picture in a girlie magazine. Nevertheless, his arousal was strong. The flesh was sensual, soft and warm to his touch. The whole body was a willing potential recipient of love favors.

She undressed him, revealing to her eyes for the first time a naked male. Its mysteries all revealed. This was not just any boy. It was Bryant, her Bryant. Nothing now to prevent them from being as close together as possible.

They did not engage in the ultimate act of love that night. They agreed it would be done in an unrushed manner in a bed without the potential for any outside distraction. Each was content to snuggle against the other, stroking and kissing body and soul. The adhering warmth was deliciously comforting and satisfying. Each touch was a new discovery. The tones of loving words lead to a meaningful peace.

Tenderness in feelings expressed through the senses is surely an apex of human ability. Body and mind seething while shrouded in a greater all-encompassing calmness.

The real wonder descended on them when they were each back in their own beds. All of the feelings lingered. A part of each was still there with the other.

12

One would think that she would be accustomed to fast moving changes in her surroundings since there had been such drastic modifications to her existence in the past. Yet, Theresa Guastella would much have preferred the dullness inherent in sameness. Her own beauty had warped her sense of judgment. Being able to have any man who fell at her feet, she had too often let herself get involved with a man unworthy of that beauty. Two men in particular had brought her to this current position of withdrawn despair. Both were handsome and dashing on the outside but devious and untrustworthy in demeanor. Taken by their overbearing attention to her, believing that they had chosen her overwhelmingly over others, it clouded her logic and perception. Once the prey is caught, interest is lost and it is on to the next conquest. The hunt is a game. They toyed with her emotions and cruelly took advantage of her. Her heart had been broken, her ego shattered. Most of all, she had lost the capacity to trust her own judgment just as she had lost faith in others. If her parents ever found out that she had an abortion, such being illegal as well, they would have disavowed her. Rather, they had taken her in believing that she was suffering the aftereffects of futile romances that needed time to heal the spirit. They did not push her to find a job or to regain a social life. They enabled her to hold her life in abeyance, to merely move with the current until she was ready to take control of the direction of her life. She loved them for that even though it was not the best thing for her. Not knowing what might be best for her, she had no impetus to think, to plan, to act.

The flowering of Rika in the past several weeks had taken the entire household by storm. Her radiance and jovial mannerisms cast an enchanting spell on them all. Fearing that any unwarranted deed, any too casual remark, might break the trance, they just heeded the direction Rika imparted. So, when Rika suggested that Theresa might double date with a friend of Bryant's, Theresa agreed although her inner being did not think it was a good idea to date anyone just yet, especially one she was forewarned was overweight and inexperienced with women. Oh well, she resigned herself to accept it as a momentary distraction, a favor for Rika. It might even feel good to give for a time rather than to merely take. Confident that she was basically a good person, it might even prove to be an opportune moment to rely on that instead of her appealing looks. The beauty would fade soon enough. Her education was limited and practical skills nonexistent. Perhaps her inner goodness would be all she might wind up with. Staring reality in the face is a bracing wake up call.

Some miles away, more like worlds apart, Phil Montague was also contemplating this impending date. Bryant had been quite convincing that he should meet Rika's sister, but Phil had his usual misgivings about it and about himself. There was little about him that he could take pride in, so what would a girl see in him that might be appealing? Nervous and unsure of himself, he always turned to eating and the weight piled on. Escape routes are not necessarily safety nets. Shriveling up in the face of his father's dictates, he could not even be his own person, whatever that might be. Not a scholar by design or choice, the only reason he got into law school was through his father's overbearing influence. He had limited romantic experiences, and the few times he got close enough to savor its impact his ineptness smothered the chance. Friends were few and merely casual as he had always been reluctant to reveal to anyone that he was so sensitive to his core. He had opened up more to Bryant than to anyone else, as he rarely talked about himself. He covered up his inadequacies and the hurts and disappointments by pretending to be the jokester. A pun here, a pun there, and feigning joviality. Avoiding extended or serious conversation at any cost. The ultimate bottom line that he thought about constantly, obsessively — really, who was he?

Bryant and Rika had discussed this potential double date at length. There was no question that it was an intrusion on their private time together but they had risen above that. There was such pride and vitality in what they had together that it should rub off on others. In a way, both Phil and Theresa were lost souls, and the common floundering might be a powerful adhesion. No guarantees, no grandiose expectations, but a chance. Certainly worth an effort in their joint opinion.

The night of the infamous double date arrived. Phil had a car, so it made it easy for them to drive over to the Guastella house. The plan was to go to a movie, a place where conversations can be minimized if awkwardness prevailed and until the acquaintance settled in. Then, they would go to Luigi's for pizza.

The evening turned out better than anticipated. Phil was entranced by Theresa's beauty and her bestowed attention on him. Theresa felt at ease with him from the start, probably because she no longer had the pressure upon herself of having to prove herself to a man. She even felt so relaxed with him that she asked him to call her Tess, a familiarity usually reserved for time-tested relationships. By evening's end, they were holding hands. Bryant and Rika basked in the accomplishment. Worthwhile deeds can come from good intentions.

After the boys had left, Theresa went to Rika's room. Rika missed the private moments with Bryant in the basement but knew they would make up for it. Full commitment means full confidence.

"It was a good evening for me," Theresa said earnestly as she stretched out on the bed.

Rika was changing into her nightgown. "You two seemed to hit it off. I am glad of that."

"Maybe I have just matured. More realistic expectations bring easier satisfactions."

"I am not sure I agree with that. Especially for dating from now on you should expect more than you received from any of your old ones."

"Maybe I did not phrase it right. I meant that I just tried to be natural and not to anticipate any special outcome. Always before I began with the premise as soon as I was attracted to him that the relationship would be the one and only."

"Phil is nice. Bryant thinks a great deal of him. He is wavering in the wind, not knowing what to do with his life and skirting what his father, a judge, demands of him. Not easy to be yourself in the face of ....".

"Other people's expectations." Theresa finished the thought as if she had started it. "That is what I meant too. Life is less of a struggle when you don't stand stubborn in the face of the onslaught. I like him. He is a funny person, and I sense he is good-natured. Not what might have attracted me before."

"Good. You both may do something for each of you."

Theresa rose and headed for the door. "Thanks, dear sister. Again, you have done more for me than I do for you."

"Who's counting. Besides, your day may come when you will need to repay any and all favors, Tess."

As Theresa headed for her room, she wondered what Rika meant by that last remark. She could do so little for herself. How could she possibly help Rika?

In the car returning to the dorm, Phil was quite jovial. "Just imagine. The prettiest girl I have ever been with, and I think she enjoyed it."

"Nothing like stating the obvious," Bryant said with a sheepish grin.

"Obviously, you did not notice that I enjoyed myself as well."

"No," Bryant feigned surprise.

"Thank you for introducing me to this angel. I actually believe I can handle it on my own from here. You were right about having someone special. It puts everything in clear focus, in its rightful place. Maybe, you should become a doctor instead of a lawyer."

"I might actually veer off and become a part time philosopher. Having Rika in my life, I earnestly believe that the most important thing for a person to achieve is to have balance in life. An assortment of accomplishments. A variety of emotional experiences. Many interests to pursue, and always to try each new undertaking as it comes along even if the old and familiar ones are the most comforting."

"The transformation kid turned into the old philosopher. Now that I am one of your disciples, I will need to dwell on all of the recent occurrences. I just hope I don't reach the quandary where you say one thing and Tess says another."

"Just another bridge waiting to be crossed."

Both remained deep in thought as they parted for their rooms. Phil crawled into bed to dream of Tess. Bryant decided to study for awhile certain the more he armed himself with the nuances of the law the closer he would get to his projected legal activist posture. The admonition of T.S. Eliot filtered into his mind — *Keep true, never be ashamed of doing right, decide on what you think is right and stick to it.*

13

Blantyre University prided itself on being a progressive institution, and it widely accepted the plaudits extended to it when it opened a free full service medical clinic for the students in 1961. Rika had not had an occasion to go there. She was healthy and rarely even caught a cold. The Guastellas also had a family doctor in town, one that had been there for all of them through the years.

Now, as she stood outside the clinic doors, she hesitated going in. She had overheard the talk about the newly approved birth control pills and that they were available at no cost to the students at the clinic. Yet, knowing about them and going in to actually request them were two different things. Her parents certainly would never approve of this, primarily for religious reasons. The moral issue would also loom large in their eyes, and she hoped that the time would not come when she might have to tell them about it. Even if she was able to explain in detail how she felt about Bryant and the excursion she wanted to take because of that love, they would argue about it and would be disappointed in her and, ultimately, blame themselves for some failure in her upbringing. The clinic kept such transactions confidential, and that made her decision easier.

With her typical resolve, she entered the clinic, and twenty minutes later she left with a three-month supply of the pills. Each month's supply was in a white oval case, each pill arranged along the perimeter with the day indicated for the daily intake. She was tempted to shout at the nurse who helped her when she saw her stare at her deformed leg and knew just what she was thinking. It is disgraceful how stupid people can be, even professional people who are supposed to know better. It is even more disgusting when they display such ignorance so openly. It hurts no less even if it could be forgiven.

This experience did give her immediate impetus to go to the *Voice* office to write the article. Bryant had given her some interesting material to include in the article if she wanted to. The writing would come easy. It was her life she was writing about. In two hours she was finished and satisfied with the content. She was eager for Bryant to read the draft.

STRAIGHT ARROW

Ex Umbris et Imaginibus in Veritem
(From shadows and symbols into the truth)
Cardinal Newman, Epitaph at Edgbaston

The Disabled — They are People Too!

Rika Guastella
and
Bryant York

The rights of so many of the members of our society are trampled upon with ease and right there before our nose. These articles have emphasized this cruel reality and have dealt with specific groups of victims. These horrendous instances of the failure of our people and our government cannot be ignored. We must recognize this for the injustice that it presents and educate ourselves about the reasons for its existence and the means to alleviate it. You must do your part with others if you can, and alone if you must, to right such persistent wrongs. Treatment of, and concepts about, the handicapped are just one tragic example. The handicapped are your brothers and sisters. They deserve no less than what others enjoy. Their limitations should be self-imposed and not predetermined by others. Even if not possible to be fully realized, the opportunities should be equal for all.

The stigma, the shame, the deviance, the negativeness, the social death of the disabled are not new. The Bible depicts handicapped as divine retribution for sinful behavior. Leviticus 21:17 says: "Whosoever that hath any blemish, let him not approach the altar to offer the bread of his God." Physical flaws negate any spiritual worthiness. The 19th Century saw the so-called "ugly laws." It was provided in the Chicago Municipal Code: "No person who is diseased, maimed, mutilated, or in any way deformed so as to be an unsightly or disgusting object or improper person to be allowed in or on the public way or other public places in this city, shall expose himself to the public view, under a penalty of not less than one dollar nor more than fifty dollars for each offense." This is how the system has looked upon and treated the handicapped!

This myth of inequality has permeated society for far too long. Flawed people are not to be pitied or scorned for their deviance from so-called normalcy. They are in fact not flawed, not adversely deviant. Any differences do not mean they are any less productive and capable to perform necessary and beneficial functions. Rather than pity, or to be institutionalized so that the problem concocted by society need not have to be dealt with, the disabled need to have self-respect which can only come from a changed attitude by business, by government, and by the people. They may need the advantage of special training, adaptable equipment, access to all places at all times, and given the opportunity to show their worth. That is not too much to ask. It is no less than they deserve.

Franklin Delanor Roosevelt knew it was not politically or culturally acceptable for him to be open about his inability to walk. Despite attempts to capture the reality of the disabled as in the 1946 movie "The Best Years of Our Lives," progress for pronouncing rights for the disabled has been arduous and minimal. With the swollen ranks of the disabled with crippled veterans from the wars and the polio epidemic, the vast numbers of deserved citizens should no longer be ignored or delayed. Movements have arisen to lead the way but much needs to be done.

It is a touch and demand of humanity that the handicapped have their rightful place in the schools, in the workforce, for housing, and in the social fabric of our communities. When you see the crippled, do not turn away from them. Pity the society that shuts them out. We are the losers. They are people too. They require love, concern and forgiveness as we all do. Their rights are symbolic of all of our rights.

14

The Saturday night before Bryant was to go home for Thanksgiving was chosen for the their love entwinement. Bryant reserved a room at a motel twenty miles away from the town. The plan was to borrow the Guastella car, and Phil would drive out the next morning to return the key and finish the checkout. A simple plan in light of the great anticipation for the grand event.

Rika lingered in the shower in preparation for the evening. Her body was alive, and she even believed there was a normal sensation in her bad leg. She so wanted to be perfect for Bryant, and desperately wanted the night to be a wonderful experience to show the man she loved that while she may not be normal in body composition she was a total woman. In a way she wanted to confirm this fact for herself as well. One of the many things that Bryant had done for her was to give her the firm belief that she could accomplish the meaningful goals in life. The total giving of herself while frightening at an earlier stage in her life now seemed like the most natural thing that she could do. Expecting never to find or feel love, it now consumed her. As the water cascaded off her slim body, it did little to cool the throbbing heat spreading along her skin. It did not bother her that she did not know exactly what to do. The one overriding asset of her found love was that there was no trepidation in whatever she might do or want. She did not have to think about what to say or what to do. She was herself, totally and completely herself. Any imperfection was pardonable. It might even be considered an affirmation of the human condition.

She chuckled to herself as she dusted herself with talcum powder. Her whole body would probably show Bryant's fingerprints. Not the crime of the century. The event of the millennium.

Tess entered through the open door as Rika was combing her hair. "Phil is taking me to dinner. Strange, I am so looking forward to it."

"I believe that often when you take a step backwards you are actually ready to move ahead."

"Totally illogical but apparently so true. Where are you off to?"

"Dad has lent us the car. We are taking a drive and spend as much time together as possible. He is going home on Wednesday for Thanksgiving."

"Does he want you to meet his parents?"

"He wants me to go home with him at Christmas, but Christmas means so much to Mom here I don't know what to do."

"You will work it out. Sounds serious. I really like him. Not that I am a good judge of character but he seems to have his feet on the ground. Easy to see that he worships you. He picked the wrong sister but I can overlook that."

"Kind person that you are. I saw him first, and I would not give him up no matter what. I haven't found a bad quality about him. I doubt if he has any. Mr. Perfect, pretty near. At one point I wondered what he sees in me. Now, I don't care. I love him and that colors everything with a rainbow."

"Lucky lady and Mr. Perfect. Quite a combination. You have my blessings, whatever that is worth."

Rika looked at her steadily. "It is worth a great deal to me."

Tess came over and kissed her on the top of the head. "I am not sure that I ever appreciated having a sister. Especially you, my dear sister. In so many ways I was more comatose than alive. My loss, as it always is."

"Mine, too. Brighter days are ahead for you. I can feel it. It is never too late to turn that proverbial corner. For both of us, our lives may be just beginning."

"I certainly do hope so. I never told anyone this before. I have been close to giving up."

"Adversity should have the opposite effect. I know that all too well. It should make you want to live life even more.....and better, much better."

"The younger sister teaching the older one."

"Not teaching. Just being practical."

"Practically teaching, then."

Both chuckled and Theresa left to get ready for her date. She felt light-headed. Grab hold of some happy moments and not worry about tomorrow. Perhaps she might have a place in this mysterious place called *LIFE* after all.

Bryant was also readying himself for this special night. His shyness was so ingrained that he wondered if it might restrict him now. No, that would not have an impact this time. He had such an overwhelming passion for Rika that it would lead him through any and all times and events. It would turn out right for them both. The newness and the freshness would serve as guideposts. A first act of love would be perfect in every way. Anticipation, so important a part towards the culmination of their union. They had weeks to look forward to the mutual surrender of virginity. Knowing that the memorable moment would arrive at their own time and pace added luster to the sweetness of it.

What are the contours, the depth of this first moment of lovemaking? There can be no universal or standard definition. No yardstick can measure it. No all-encompassing term or phrase can describe it in all of its dimensions and sensations. It is one of those rare events in life that must be experienced. The feelings must roam through the system uninhibited. It needs to be absorbed to the very foundation of one's being. It has to be filtered through each pore in the body and digested in diverse ways. Each nerve and tendon is inflamed. Indescribable and unforgettable.

The motel room was nothing special but would not detract from their desired end. Once inside the door, Rika rested the cane against the wall. They shed their coats and embraced. The kiss was tender, the touch of tongues kinetic.

Bryant was the first to speak. His voice was gentle just as Rika knew it would be, and knowing that his touch in the moments to come would match the strains of his voice. "I knew this moment would arrive. Now that it is here, I want it to last and last."

"It will my love. Special moments are forever. As we give to each, the meaning and memory of it will endure."

"If I was listening to such dialogue in a movie, I would think it awfully corny. Living it adds a particular glow."

"I have only disdain for those who pity me for my absence of so-called normality. I pity others who have no love."

Bryant removed the coverlet from the bed and pulled the sheet down. They slowly undressed each other. Naked body against naked body in a hug of tender force.

He carried her to the bed. She looked deep into his eyes. "Turn off the light if you do not want to look at my leg. I really won't mind."

"You turn off the light if you do not want to see me salivating over your beautiful body."

Rika smiled. "Do you ever say the wrong thing?"

"I want you to hang around long enough to hear my many blunders. Besides, I want to see your expression. It is part of the total experience."

In the comfort of the bed as their clinging bodies warmed to their touch, the expression of love was patient and satisfying. Rika told him that he need not take any special caution with her leg, and she only regretted that she could not wrap both legs around him to hold him firmly within her. Her body tingled with each caress, each light kiss. He held back on his ultimate exertion as long as he could hoping to maximize her pleasure. He did not withdraw, and their panting, perspiring bodies stuck together as an obvious symbol of the bond.

Later, she caressed his manhood to alertness and they made love again. Her sigh spoke volumes. A kiss capped the rising adventure. They dozed, bodies and minds at ease. Surely, it was their moment in the sun.

15

The Yorks waited for their son at Grand Central Station. The train was twenty minutes late, but it was a busy travel day and delays were common. They waited in silence. There was not much to talk about these days. They no longer compared their involvement at the school and everything else progressed in a near silent carrier of habit. They were in agreement that they would try to influence Bryant to look at his romance as a first one and that it should be a learning experience as others will develop upon which he could build and appreciate more. It seemed completely logical from their perspective.

Frieda often pondered the loss of the depth of feelings in long marriages, hers in particular. There was not much sense in trying to place the blame for it. It was just a fact. In a new marriage there is much giving, much notice and appreciation of the giving. The longer the marriage the more the taking aspect takes over. Moments of thought and consideration more difficult to execute and barely noticed when present. She could also not control the attraction she had developed for Martin Ornstein, a new teacher at the school. He had to be at least ten years her junior, but the more she studied his mannerisms she had grown to admire and respect his rapport with the students. She was finding it more difficult to repress her ardor. It

91

was a fantasy that had come to sustain her. She looked forward to each new day at the school, and her dreams took on a new dimension. It added a teasing vitality to an otherwise rather dull and monotonous life. One of the longstanding disappointments had been that she had never developed a close friendship with another woman. It would be so satisfying to share these feelings with another person. While her life was not completely empty, it could be so much fuller.

Riding the subway back to the apartment, Bryant gave his parents an earful about Rika. They both were amazed at how much he talked, and with such animation. The boy and the man had merged. Both knew it was going to make their planned approach more difficult. A thin line often separates the role of advisor from the position of opposer.

Back in his old room, a flood of warm feelings and memories immersed Bryant in deep thought. Here was a part of his being that was so meaningful before law school. Now it seemed so distant, almost preparatory for the long march he had undertaken. His new vision had taken hold of him completely. He was that sure of his destiny. He had never been so confident about anything else in his life.

He spent two hours on the telephone with Rika that evening. There was always so much to talk about, including events and observations past and plans ahead. Each thought brought on its own exposition, its own direction. By holding one close to your heart that person is always near to you. Hearts in sync never sink.

That night, after his parents had gone to bed, Bryant sat at his old desk, the desk that had been his studies companion, and wrote a short story.

A Lesson Learned Too Late

There is a moment that arrives in our lives when regret turns into understanding........if we are lucky. To brood about the past is unproductive. Most of us would probably make the same mistakes again, if in fact they were mistakes. More often than not, they were merely a choice of actions that turned out poorly. Hard to figure, harder to swallow. By studying the action and the reaction, even a mistake can be flipped to show a positive side.

For this poor soul as he lay upon his deathbed, he realized far too late that regret had eaten away at him and had turned him into a bitter old man. He had known from an early age that worrying about something in advance was the worst thing he could do, but somehow it was overcompensated by the worrying afterwards that the wrong decision or action had been taken.

So what had gone so terribly wrong that he could not fix it or, at least, lessen its impact? What was the monumental mistake that he had made that haunted him all of his remaining days and that overshadowed any positive element that crept into his existence? It was only at this last moment when his breath was short and labored that he understood that life is really a series of compromises. We give up something to gain something else. If the gain proves unsatisfactory in the light of what has been given up, effort should be doubled to correct or diminish its effect. It can be as simple as that if emotional entanglement does not burden the analysis. Surely, one can recoup some of what has been lost. A creative and flexible mind might be able to sort through the result and make do with the outcome or channel it towards a more worthwhile end.

The remorse grew painfully over the years after he decided to put his mother in the institution. With a bit more resolve, he might have been able to keep her with him for a couple of more years even though it would have been at great personal sacrifice. As the agony took hold and festered in his soul, it led to losing the only woman he had ever loved, dissatisfaction with any occupation or workplace situation, and a turning away from people and things that he might enjoy. The nervous twitch that developed was the constant reminder of his moment of weakness and of the torment raking his being.

The two years before she died in that terrible place, a place where he had thrust her among people more dangerous and far sicker than she was. It was not better for her, and it turned out as a disaster for him. He had institutionalized himself in the same act, and he became the victim of a guilt that shredded his composition. He could not live in peace with himself. The proof all too evident as he lay here on this bed dying slowly and not one person cared enough to be there with him.

Instead of regretting his deed, he should have just admitted openly that he had made a mistake and learned from it so that he might exhibit more tolerance and flexibility with others. The best way for him to have made it up to her would have been for him to make a better life for himself because of his errant decision. A happy life would have been the compensation for her suffering. She had instilled in him virtues that could have been nurtured and refined. He could have helped himself by helping others. He could have and should have. The regret should have been a start and not an end. A string of regrets that he had hung himself with. Now, only death would help him. Death for a wasted life. A pity for him. A lesson for the rest of us.

16

Stuffed from the Thanksgiving feast, the Yorks settled in the living room. This was the time planned by the parents for broaching the subject of Bryant and his newfound love. There had been many talks over the years. Bryant had been considered an adult and a contributing member of the family since his early teens, and the blending of the parent and teacher roles had led to frank and serious discussions.

Carl, resting comfortably in his favorite armchair, broke the silence. "Son, I know you appreciate that your mother and I have always had your best interests at heart. We want to talk to you about your relationship with Rika. We consider ourselves quite progressive and hold nothing against her, believe that. You are our son, and it is you that we are most concerned with. We are very proud of you and what you have become. We read the articles you write and boast to others about them. That law school has become so appealing is very gratifying. We admire your desire to become a legal advocate for the downtrodden. What we want to make sure is that you keep everything in true focus. When there are many facets at play pulling you in different directions it is often difficult to see the merit of each factor and the lasting importance of decisions. Rika is really your first girl friend, and you are relatively inexperienced with romantic involvements. She is handicapped, and your large heart I am sure encompasses that in what you feel for her. That should not dictate a goal in your professional life that might foreclose other options, especially ones that might prove far more lucrative. There is no escaping the reality that financial success can lead to a very comfortable life. You should not get swept up in a cause that also spills over into a serious relationship with a person merely because that person is an object of the cause. I guess what I am trying to say, no matter how disjointed it may sound, is that to make hasty decisions makes it harder to achieve the right balance in your life. Experiences and expectations, particularly first exposures to a future career path or in romance, are more like building blocks. The more you have the more flexibility you have in arranging them and the stronger the structure that you can erect." He paused long enough to discern Frieda's slight smile of encouragement. "Rika may be the most wonderful girl in the world, but you owe it to yourself to date others and expose yourself to an array of social situations to be sure of that. We are not prejudiced or predisposed to like or dislike anyone, especially because of their differences. Yet, life is difficult under the best of conditions. To be with a person who has some physical or even a mental limitation is a constant presence in whatever you might do, wherever you may go. It is a long-term restraint. It would always impact you as a person, your future, your children."

Bryant had expected a lecture about Rika. After all, these were his parents and their perspective was different. They had been protective of him all of his life, and he did not expect them to stop being that way now. Parental love is a strong phenomenon. It is not always understanding and tolerant. It is, however, deep and abiding. It deserves respect even if in a particular instance it is misguided. Bryant would be a parent himself someday, and he hoped he could do as well as his parents had done with him. On close analysis, he was not sure they were successful as a couple but they were good parents. He rarely observed affection between them. Yet, they had always been affectionate with him. Not necessarily hugs and kisses but a reassuring pat, a soft look, a gentle smile. Even knowing the subject would be broached, he was not quite sure how his response would be received.

"Mom, Dad, we have had many talks in the past. I am sure there will be more in the future. I know you mean well, and that is why I will always listen and respect what you have to say. When I left for Blantyre, there were many uncertainties for me to face. Most of all, I had to confront my own fears, my inadequacies. I have always felt socially inadequate. My experience with girls was very limited, as you know so well, and my imagination blotted out reality. That all changed when I met Rika. She is a beautiful person, and that far outshines whatever imperfection her body might have. In fact, her condition has made her a much wiser and feeling individual. I realize that the giving of love is the greatest gift one can give. She has given me that, without reserve, without the slightest hesitation or qualification. Through that giving of herself, it supports the sense that I have developed that my future belongs to helping those that a society shuns. She and I are a perfect match. Together we contemplate what has to be done and proceed to do it. Accomplishments that might not be possible if either one of us acted alone. Whether we ultimately marry or not does not detract from the fact for now we need each other and want to be together. I hope to bring her home with me for a couple of days over Christmas. I know she will love you, and I am hoping you will give yourselves a chance as a matter of intellect and fairness to love her. She means a great deal to me. I love her, and that should be enough for you to accept her on that basis."

Frieda rose and hugged him. "My dear son. We are tolerant and progressive people. We are sure she is everything you say she is. We also know that you are young and inexperienced. Different experiences and the passing of time are what bring all of the colors to the future that we face. Be with her, love her, just don't think in terms of ultimates or absolutes. Undoubtedly, you are doing as much for her as you say she has done for you. Fine. Relationships worth having are all composed of that kind of give and take. Just don't foreclose other possibilities, other friendships, other business or social alliances. Do not turn away from other romantic involvements. They will place current situations in clearer perspective. That is all we are trying to say. We will, of course, welcome her here at Christmas because she is your friend, just as our home is open to all people who find a place in your life, temporary or permanent. We whole-heartedly support the professional goal you aspire to, even if it may not be as financially attractive as other possibilities, but again you should leave all of the doors open before you. Life can hold an abundance of surprises, and it is not until the moment that we confront them do we know how or when direction may change." She paused for an instant, just long enough for the thought to penetrate to her heart that she was also addressing her own outlook. "Above all, we want you to know that we are always here for you. Our futures are intertwined. Your victories and disappointments are ours as well. Your wife will be our daughter, your children our children. Our fondest wish is for you to be happy and to be fulfilled. We will bask in such an achievement."

Bryant understood their position and probably would have taken the same stance in their place. At some future time, he might well face a similar dilemma with his own children. Yet, for this moment there was a generational gap that prevented him from abiding by their words. They could not understand the intricacies of his being and his feelings. It would be best just to be appreciative of their commendable intentions and to keep their words in mind while he exercised his very own intellect and spirit as being what he had to rely on the most. Experience ought to be a part of that. Who is to say, however, that the first experience might not be the truest and most important one? Who can say with certainty that a first exposure might not be the most important, the most ever-lasting? Who can say that a first love might not be the only love ever worth having?

He hugged them both. "I will keep in mind all that you have said. Trust me to be who I am, the who that you helped to create, and to do in the final analysis only what I am convinced is right."

End of talk, end of discussion. A family communicating, a family together. Each taking from it a slightly different variation of the content and accomplishment.

17

On the drive back to Blantyre, Phil had much to think about. The talk he had with his father went far better than he thought it would. In retrospect, he should not have dreaded it so much. He came away with a new respect for his father, and a better feeling about himself. In fact, he even had the impression that his father appreciated his candidness. In reply to the uncertainty of his future, his father downplayed him becoming a lawyer. He merely suggested that since Phil was not sure where or what he wanted, that he stay in law school and get a law degree. It would be a plus on any road he wished to travel. He might even get used to the idea of the law by then. If not, many people in the business world profit from a law degree even if they have never practiced. If nothing else, it gives one a keen power of observation, the ability to accumulate and categorize facts, and the reasoning to find solutions to problems.

The more he thought about it the more sense it all seemed to make. It would preserve his options while not standing still. The added benefit was that he would still be near Tess to see where this relationship would settle out. How could he not be taken with such a beautiful woman with such a gentle mannerism? She looked at him steadily whenever they were together, her eyes sparkling when he would speak. This was a rare experience for him as he was generally used to being ignored and frowned upon. She was attentive and affectionate, attributes he could only have dreamt about. She was always reaching for his hand to hold as if the clasp was truly meaningful for her. Instead of repelling his embraces and kisses, she fostered them by moving close to him and staying that way inviting further and more intimate contact. He was sure she would let him make love to her but his ineptness made him wary. He had not even attempted to touch her in any inappropriate way. He did not want to do anything that might shock her or disappoint her. She was a lifeline for him to hold fast to if troubled waters lay ahead. She evidently enjoyed having a bumbling idiot slobber all over her. He was more than ready to oblige. Between her attraction to him and his father's placid advice, Phil felt a bolt of self-confidence that could be used as a shield and easily converted to a weapon.

Of course, no amount of preparation or anticipation could have readied him for what she told him that night after he arrived back. Throughout dinner at a local restaurant, she was pleasant enough. He relived through her exposition all of the Thanksgiving dinner and her new found significance of family and being an active participant in the gatherings. Her brother even joined them with a new girlfriend, although he nervously left right after the eating. She listened carefully as he described the discussion with his father, and she felt good for him about such a major accomplishment. He sensed a change, almost an imperceptible one, and he hoped he was wrong.

After dinner they drove to a secluded spot just outside of town and parked. She was distant, and even in the darkness he could see that she was looking well beyond the car. "Anything wrong?" he asked nervously.

"Not with you," she responded in a faint voice. "I thought about you over Thanksgiving. I need to do the right thing for you."

"Here it comes," he thought. *The kiss of death.*

"I have grown very fond of you. I am not used to men like you. No pretensions, no deception. For that, I owe you that I be completely honest with you. You need to know what I have done and who I really am. I hope you can handle it. I hope you will not look down on me because of it."

She paused not so much waiting for a response from him but more to gather her thoughts and the courage to put them into words. "Nobody else knows about what I am going to tell you, not even my family. I trust that it will remain solely with you." Another pause to muster the strength to say what she convinced herself she had to say. "My beauty has been a curse. It made it far too easy for me to be popular. I did not have to do anything to earn it. Just smile, and people noticed and wanted to get close. It also made me susceptible to being steered in the wrong direction by people who pretended to worship that beauty. I listened to the wrong people, thinking that because they were so interested in me, so attentive to me, that they would lead me to places and things exciting and fulfilling. How wrong I was! All it did was to make me weak, to cloud my vision, and make me prey to the devices of others for their own selfish and greedy purposes. I was a bad judge of character, for sure. Two dishonest men crossed into my life. I was taken by their worldliness, their gushing compliments, and a torrent of empty phrases feigning affection. Promises proved false and misleading. I was manipulated for their own design and pleasure. It is not easy to admit what a fool I was, and I paid dearly for my blunders. Basically, I have no one to blame except myself. I let it happen, not really understanding the reason for my actions or the consequences. I became pregnant and had an illegal abortion. Scary, painful, and worst of all I was all alone. I have not fully gotten over this episode in my life. I am still at the point where I am afraid to feel too much for and about others. I still do not think I can trust my actions or my judgment. I have so much yet to learn about myself and my world."

He did not say anything. It was painfully obvious he had not been prepared to hear such a disclosure.

"I will understand completely if you do not want to see me again," she continued in a weak voice. "You have your own problems, and probably the last thing you need is to have my messed up life to deal with. I wish I had an ounce of Rika's strength. I have gone full circle from feeling sorry for her to envying her. Overcoming obstacles does build character. It has probably come too late for me. I am trying to be a good person, trying to build myself up. I understand that I must be the first person to help me. I would like you to be there for me as I do this. Again, I will not hate you for not sharing such a burden."

Phil was not silent because of the revelation. He was quiet as he assessed his own reaction to it. Here was a beautiful woman baring her soul to him because she cared enough about him to be open and honest with him. It struck him with great significance. As a person who had shielded his own sensitivities with surface humor, the seriousness of her travail struck a much appreciated responsive chord. Before he spoke, he embraced her and noted the trembling of her body. A touch of irony as he recalled the discussion he had with Bryant where he had advised him not to get involved with a girl with special problems of her own. For an overeater, it was humbling to eat his own words.

When he finally did speak, it was with a voice that surprised him. An inner strength, perhaps because he was now at peace with himself and with his father, found its way to produce a steady, secure tone. "Tess, I am touched by your taking me into your confidence. I am the last person in the world to judge you for what you have done. I have wrestled with my own demons all of my life with little to brag about or to get excited over. I think highly of you, and especially admire your frank outpouring. I think you are unduly harsh with yourself. Mistakes are there for us to learn from them and to fortify our conviction to go on. I see that so clearly now. You are welcome, very welcome to lean on me whenever you need or want to. It is probably more of our leaning on each other. We will both be better off if together we can find the will to improve and find a true purpose in life. I am sure of that. You have done nothing that I need to forgive you for. I think you have punished yourself long enough. Turn the corner and concentrate on what is ahead. The world surely needs the sensitivity you have revealed to me. The way to do that will emerge if you just give it a chance. I will be right at your side, if you will allow me to share that promising end."

Tess hugged him tightly. "Dearest, Phil. I would like nothing more. I would like to be at your side as well. I just know that you will be doing wonderful things."

"Once I would have doubted that. Now, I see a sunrise instead of a sunset."

18

Thanksgiving had been a revealing moment for Jean Guastella as well. Rika and Tess helped with all of the preparations for the feast, and the levity was pronounced and contagious. The relaxed demeanor of her daughters and their banter relieved any tension that might otherwise have filled the air. She could not recall laughing so much, and it felt good, very good. Even Bernie came to the dinner with a new girlfriend, and they all thought she was charming and hoped that she might be a good influence on him. Now that Rika was absorbed with a young man, Jean felt a great deal of weight had been lifted from her shoulders. She did not have to focus on Rika constantly. It broadened the family outlook considerably. At the dinner her attention flitted between all of her children and her sense of family was fortified. She spoke equally to all of them, hugged them all numerous times. It was the best Thanksgiving she had ever had.

That night in bed, even though quite tired, she turned to Salvo and looked at him with renewed appreciation. He had always been there, comforting and supporting her motherly role. It was a stark revelation to admit to herself that she could not have done it all without him. It was even more pointed to recognize that the passionless marriage was not his doing but originated with her. She had used

Rika's dependency as a convenient way for her to put everything else aside except her imagination. It was long overdue for her to return to reality, to pay a form of homage to the man who stuck by her and gave of himself more than she had given. Rika's discovery of love led her to realize that the love she imagined she deserved was right here all of the time. She reached out for him. "My sweet husband. My dearest man. Forgive me for neglecting you and us. Thank you for being so patient with me. I love you very much."

Salvo did not respond. It was a gift from heaven. He had given up on ever recovering the love of their early days, the days when without many material possessions they were able to fortify their existence by just being together and taking pleasure in that simple fact. He turned to her and clutched her in an embrace that flooded his soul with the fondest of memories. They slept peacefully, bodies interlocked.

Rika lay in her bed, a thousand thoughts and feelings flooded her mind and body. She missed Bryant to her very core, longing for his kisses and tender touches. The uncanny feeling that he made her whole and yet she was in parts, and when not together a part of her was with him. Loving him was the most natural act for her. Being loved by him was a joy beyond description.

Two days later, they were reunited. In a perfect world, and if she was in near-perfect physical condition, she would have rushed into his arms. Rika had to be content with Bryant rushing to her. That was not so bad. She had an instant to study the excitement on his face and to revel in the feeling of love swooping down on her. She waited on the porch, anticipating the reunion as a very private matter. The kiss was special and it enveloped them both with the security they had generated with their togetherness. She had waited long enough so the cold had seeped into her bones. Now she did not notice anything except the force of a love that ignited her very essence.

For Bryant, it was a telling moment as well. Their temporary separation was bearable only because it was so brief. The reassurance of the togetherness was as he had expected. Most boys would not give Rika a second look. They could not see what he saw, could not sense the depth and great emotional capacity of this frail looking person. Her handicap made all of her other qualities burst with power. How truly fortunate he was to have found love with such a wonderful girl. Even through their coats, the vibrations of the magnetism between them was felt and coveted.

"My sweet man," she whispered.

"My beloved woman," he responded in her ear.

She removed her glasses so her cheek could rest fully against his. Such a simple gesture, such a basic action, all adding to bliss. "Let's not ever be apart again."

"My plan exactly."

As the days passed, the one aspect that became somewhat unsettling was their increasing role as student activists. It raised concern and a degree of anguish. Their articles were increasingly popular and were reprinted in a number of college papers across the country. A mixture of pressures emerged. The more reactionary student groups wanted even stronger articles against the war and an outright call for overt action by students. The University, through the newspaper's faculty advisor, requested that the tenor and messages of the articles be toned down. With the war becoming more and more of a possibility every day, with the draft gearing up to induct thousands of young men to possibly fight a war on foreign soil thousands of miles away where American interests were negligible, Bryant and Rika knew what they had to say. And what they had to say would not sit well with certain factions in the University and in the nation. Their straight arrow needed to target the truth as they saw it and felt compelled to tell it. After all, young people have ideals. They have principles and dreams. They are entitled to make their own way in this thing called life and not see it brought to a premature end for some unreasoned and unnecessary cause.

Rika's growing fear was that student deferments might be dropped and that Bryant might be drafted. He would have to fight in a war he did not believe in, possibly to be killed. Young blood to be spilled and all those dreams smashed. No matter what was to happen, their personal situation was caught up in the larger turmoil. Trying times demand leaders, some who might in their quieter moments wish otherwise.

> *To know how to say what other*
> *people may think, is what makes*
> *men poets and sages: and to dare*
> *to say what others only dare to*
> *think, makes men martyrs or reformers.*

Elizabeth Rundle Charles

Added to their very special relationship, to the individual tie was this mutual commitment to a higher purpose. A cause to espouse to preserve the values of the nation and to avoid losses that would never be undone. It grew stronger with each passing day. Small as they were, the shadow they cast loomed longer and longer. Today it might be in the universities. Tomorrow, it would be to the villages, the cities, and the enclaves of all America.

Straight Arrow

Ex Umbris et Imaginibus in Veritatem
(From shadows and symbols into the truth)
Cardinal Newman, Epitaph at Edgbaston

by

Rika Guastella
and
Bryant York

The sabers are rattling. Powerful interests in this country, for their own greedy and misguided benefit, are intent on leading us into a full-scale war in Vietnam. Young men are to be drafted by the thousands. Sons and brothers torn from family units, separated from their plans, their expectations, and their hopes. Sending them to a far off land to fight and possibly die for concocted and vague ideological reasons is wrong, deadly wrong. The loss of one American life under such circumstances would be a tragedy. Any such life could be tomorrow's Albert Einstein, Jonas Salk, or Franklin Delanor Roosevelt. Any life is a flower taken before it buds. It would leave gaping holes in the lives of loved ones and in our society. Such spilled blood would cover the globe in its propensity and scar the planet.

Before any of this happens, it is imperative that we voice our concerns, our outrage. Oppose this war! Write and visit your congressmen, join demonstrations, and express your views to whoever will listen. Do not waste any opportunity to express yourselves. There is too much at stake here to be complacent.

The voices out there are growing against this war. Listen to the words, ponder the ideas. Our best and maybe only hope is in the force of prevailing numbers. Fill the streets. Shout from the rooftops. If nonviolent means do not work, seek other ways to exert maximum influence. It may be our only chance. We are in this together and united we must remain.

It is time to reject and act against the August 1964 Gulf of Tonkin Resolution passed by the Congress which is so vaguely worded that it gives President Johnson permission to take whatever military step he wants to in North or South Vietnam.

The May movement of 1964 has been founded to counteract the imperialistic actions of the US Government. A United States invasion of Vietnam serves no purpose but to gain more power and to repress the Vietnamese people.

A march in Washington against the war is planned for December 14th. A bus has been chartered that will leave Blantyre the night before and travel all night to the march. It will be joined by many buses from universities all across the land. It is time for us to take a stand and to be heard in a show of *unity and single purpose. We'll see you on the bus!*

19

While alone in the school office for a few moments, Frieda York pulled Martin Ornstein's file from the active faculty drawer of the massive file cabinet. When she read that he was married and had two children that was all she needed to know. In spite of her yearning and strong attraction to the young man, she could not see herself as a home wrecker. The wife and children would not be subject to any emotional anguish caused by her. Frieda had kept so much to herself over the years, a little more repressed yearning would not be anything new. Yet, each time he came into the school office he did not fail to smile at her with that beguiling grin and to inquire about the progress of her day. Her stomach would quiver, and she was sure the blood rushed to her cheeks. To blush as a young girl might.

The early December snowstorm caught everyone by surprise. Rarely were the city schools called off because of inclement weather. Most of the students were able to walk to school. Those that did not walk took the subway. The same was true for the majority of the teachers. Since they had no car, Frieda and Carl rode the subway. On that day when all were caught unprepared, Frieda happened to be alone in the office. The other staff people by coincidence called in sick or took leave because of the weather. Norm Ornstein entered the office just as he did so many times before. His smile was impish.

"Hey, Frieda, are you the sole greeter today?"

She barely was able to find her voice to respond. "Yes." Just gazing on his face twisted her usual smooth demeanor into a knot.

"Makes it and you special for the day. But then again, you are special every day."

"Thank you, kind sir. Is your class light today?"

"Sure is. Just a handful of the little gremlins. I left them doing deskwork. No sense proceeding with a lesson plan that I will just have to repeat tomorrow. Is Carl here?"

She tried valiantly to regain complete composure. "Yes. He'll go on today as if they were all here. It will be their problem to catch up. He believes in that instead of dragging them up. Sort of swim or sink in their own juices."

"Sounds like one tough fellow. A bit harsh as I see it. I am from the new education school, I suppose. A teacher needs to be flexible if he wants the students to be able to bend."

"He is strict. Part of the old-fashioned school. Old dogs do not learn new tricks."

"Is he an old-fashioned husband as well?"

Not knowing how to interpret the question, she hesitated for a moment before answering. "I really never thought about it in those terms. I suppose he is."

"Sorry. I did not mean to pry or to get personal." He paused and then corrected himself just as if he were talking to his students and had caught himself stating something he really did not mean to say. "No. I did mean to get personal. I meant it when I said you are very special, and I just associate that status with you deserving special treatment."

He moved closer to the desk, and she was sure that he could see her trembling. His statement quickly confirmed that. "You are shivering. Are you cold?"

"No," she stammered.

"You are not afraid of me, are you?"

"No, I am afraid of me."

He sat down on the corner of the desk at which she was sitting and daringly covered her hand with his. The touch excited her and sent quakes through her entire system. Anybody passing by in the hall could look through the glass door and see plainly what was going on. The risk only added to the intensity of her excitement. This had to rank among the most thrilling moments of her life.

The feel of his hand was warm and gentle. She looked deeply into his wide brown eyes, knowing he was relishing being able to toy with her. "You shouldn't be doing this," she finally managed to say in a weak voice.

"Do you want me to take my hand away?"

"No," her voice barely audible.

"Come with me to the storeroom." He did not wait for any response but gently tugged her to her feet and led her to the adjoining room where the teacher supplies were kept. Shutting the door behind them, he put his arms around her and softly kissed her on the lips. A near-silent moan escaped from her mouth. He kissed her again, this time with increasing passion. His tongue entered her mouth, and a hand went to her breast and clutched it through her dress. She returned the kiss with mounting ardor. Her body was aflame, ignited by a spark of desire long dormant. His embrace was robust and she could not remember Carl ever holding her with such ardor.

They did not speak. Kiss followed kiss, each as sweet as the one before it. He nibbled at her ear, kissed her tenderly on the nape of her neck by moving the collar of the dress aside. He unbuttoned the front of her dress and moved his hand along the flesh just above her breasts. She was sure her skin would burn his hand. "This is wrong," she kept telling herself even though she was powerless to stop it or even to retard his advances. Her nipples became erect and she longed for more of his touch. He kissed her cleavage, and snuggled his nose deep into it. She wished she had not worn any undergarments that day. He then kissed her again deeply on the lips and buttoned up her dress. "Not here and now. I have wanted you since the first time I saw you. You are a magnificent woman, and I am putty in your hands." He kissed her on the cheek lightly and left the room.

She was weak in the knees and barely stumbled back to her desk. After drawing several deep breaths, she faced the realization that she was not the same woman that she was fifteen minutes before. The feel of him was full upon her, and one impulse emerged clearly. When he would tell her where they would meet, she would be there. After all, what would she be giving up?

Frieda's eyes popped open. It had all been just a dream but such a sweet one at that. So real and making her feel so alive. The warmth in her loins would not subside and she languished in the bed feasting on the aftermath of her reverie. It mattered little for the moment that it was a love and a life she would never have.

20

The first snowfall fell upon the Blantyre campus bringing wonder and awe to all who grasped its majesty. A silent blanket of white, accentuating shapes, covering blemishes, and presenting an entirely new version of old sights. The crunch of the new snow under Bryant's boots was the only sound he heard as he walked back to the dormitory. For his overactive mind, it was not just a sound. It was another symbol of how mankind was being crunched. It represented in each individual step a distinctive mark of people buried under foot.

Back at the dorm, he stopped by Phil's room. Phil was much more serious since his dating of Tess and the Thanksgiving talk with his father. The involvement and the understanding were working wonders. Not only was there a more concentrated immersion in his studies, his outlook was so much more positive.

"Bryant, good to see you. I was starting to think that your celebrity status made you feel too good for your old friends."

"Only friends would appreciate my celebrity role."

Phil chuckled. "The greatest thing that law school has done for me so far is to force me to grow up. I used to look on the possibility of a struggle as an inconvenience. Now I see it as a frame of reference. It is a standard by which to measure and associate with other struggles, other people. In any struggle there may be fewer choices but they are clearer somehow. As my guru, you should have told me all of this."

"Would you have believed me?"

"Probably not."

"I keep learning things of my own each day. Life looks different through your own eyes and experience rather than relying on the views of others."

"True. Yet, it is only when you try to see how others perceive what happens to them can you understand why they react the way that they do."

"My sights reveal that a philosopher is emerging in you."

"I cannot let you travel through such mysteries on your own, can I?"

Bryant patted him on the shoulder before he turned to leave. "I welcome the company."

He was going to tell him about the meeting that he just had with the Dean of the Law School, Dean Hodgkins. He thought better of it, as it really only involved him and perhaps Rika. Dean Hodgkins had been firm when he pronounced in so many words that unless Bryant stopped writing such inciting articles there would be no room for him in the law school. The Dean had intimated that a lawyer's role in society is as guardian of the dictates of government and to ease people into following the decisions made and rules effectuated. There was no leeway for the right of free speech that Bryant asserted in the total picture. He was lucky to have even gotten that argument in, and the Dean dismissed him with a wave of the hand. These surely were difficult times, and there would be some dire consequences for him personally. He wondered how his parents would react if he was dropped from the school. Then, there was the possibility that it would catapult him to the front of the draft line. There would be no problem with Rika's reaction, of that he was certain. Yet, her parents might look upon him in a different light. Where would he go? How could he be away from Rika? Now that he truly recognized the value of having ideals, could he abandon them? Would he be stooping to the will of the societal demands that he was fighting against?

In his room, to calm his agitated mind, he decided to write a story. Then he would face the prospect of what the near future would hold for him and if it even was worth to study that evening.

FREE FLOAT

As she gazed out upon the water, she tried to clarify her position. A peaceful setting was supposed to help unclutter the mind and enable one to focus on what really matters. This was, perhaps, the nub of her problem. What was really important? If she could have it all then it would not be necessary to prioritize. She would not have to make choices. Was that realistic? Was it all possible? Could she live life without a safety net?

The one theory that kept emerging was that young people have been planning more for the short-term than the long haul. Now that she had graduated from high school, if she wanted to go to college it would have to be by borrowing the money or working her way through. The thought of either alternative did not frighten her, but as long as she had no idea what she wanted to study would it make any sense at this point? Then, there was her family. Her parents were embittered by the divorce proceedings, and as much as they pressured her she refused to choose between them. Her so-called friends were fickle and flighty. None of them wanted to have a serious conversation. Boys, clothes, makeup, and pop music were the limit of their experience and motivation. Not the least was her inability to communicate clearly and forcefully enough so that others would actually listen to her. On top of all of this was a basic fear that others would take undue advantage of her.

Off in the distance she saw a small boat moving ever so slowly through the water. What struck her about it was that its progress was steady. She wished she could emulate that boat and move in a direction of her choosing and not be concerned with how slow the progress might be to the destination. Maybe this boat did not actually have a place it was aiming for but merely gliding effortlessly through the water until some port of refuge came into view. Could she just float in the great open space until a goal prompted her to seek a place to land? Not very practical and difficult to explain but certainly an attractive option until she made up her mind about developments.

She shook her head. No, it would be just postponing the anguish. She was already adrift. It was just then that the clarity of looking far in the distance coalesced with her own being. She had to maximize her independence from family, friends, and the female stereotype expectancies. She would join the Free People's Commune in Montana. Communes are utopian communities. The notion of collective living is emphasized as a form of self-fulfillment and personal growth. By withdrawing from the larger social fabric, a commune is an alternative to the way things are dictated. It would be just right for her! A peaceful lagoon on which to free float.

21

It may have been the impact of their article, or just the propelling events on the national and world scene, there wound up being three chartered buses from Blantyre to the anti-war march in Washington. The buses traveled during the night to be there for the 8:00 a.m. march assembly. Before settling into slumber, the students sang repeatedly all of the anti-war and protest songs they could think of — *Study War No More, Blowin' in the Wind, Tear Down the Wall, We Shall Overcome, Where Have All the Flowers Gone,* and *If I Had a Hammer.* Rika rested her head on Bryant's shoulder, contentment and sense of purpose spreading all over her.

Thousands rallied at the steps of the Capitol, amassing for the march to the Washington Monument. Old and young, from all walks of life, to protest any involvement by a peace-loving nation in an unnecessary war. Arm-in-arm, reaching the breadth of the streets, a unity in spirit and design. *"HELL NO, WE WON'T GO!"* A chant for all of the public officials to sit up and take notice that this would be an unpopular war and that the will of the people was against it. The slow moving mass easily allowed Rika to keep up. Other disabled persons were in the throng, some in wheelchairs. An additional affinity, bolstering principles for the moment as well as far and beyond this momentous event. A steady flow of humanity to accentuate and glorify peace and all facets of the human family.

It was not until the ride back to the University that they discussed the threatening pronouncement the Dean had given. As tired as they were, the issue had to be addressed and resolved. Hands clasped brought unanimity of thought. To remove the immediate repercussion, it was decided that the articles would just carry Rika's name even though they both would write them. If that did not succeed to ward off the possibility of adverse action, or if a similar edict would be forthcoming towards Rika from the Dean of the Liberal Arts School, then the articles would continue with no byline or with fictitious names. They doubted that the newspaper itself would be threatened as that would certainly compound the situation and might well draw unwarranted attention to the course of events. With the new found maturity their relationship had been graced with, they would take each step in progression and hope that the cause would force the abandonment of any punitive actions.

They snuggled together on the seat. The touch of bodies was an added comfort to the touching of their ideas and ideals. Bryant recalled the other night when they dozed naked in each other's arms. His love for Rika had risen far above the physical aspect, although that was important and pleasurable. He cared for and about her. The sharing of thoughts, the words and touches of an accommodating attitude, bundled together as an answer to what love is. It is not just one component of a relationship. It is the combination of many facets of a telling life joined with another's. It is not staid, not fixed in one place or pointed in only one direction. It is flexible enough to adapt to the demands of the moment, the needs of both persons. As long as each tries to be patient and understanding, the relationship is sturdy and will endure. That was his wish for them, and he had the feeling that this was one wish that would not go whoosh.

They had discussed a number of times the concept of a first love being an only love. The newness, the freshness, the initial upsurge in passion might lead many experiencing a first love to think that such is the one and only. More often than not, however, it is just the first exposure upon which a later relationship is to be based on and compared with. Yet, there are the exceptions when all of the pieces fit together just right and where the bond is so secure that it cannot be dislodged. Because of, or in spite of, their late emergence on the dating front, both Bryant and Rika felt strongly that this was all they could ever want from love or a relationship with another person. It was not just the attraction and the passion in their lovemaking, or merely the comfort level they enjoyed as a couple, it was the complete compatibility of their togetherness, the overlap of ideals and expectations. It was as they termed it, the marvel of their twosome.

22

Carl and Frieda knew this moment was crucial. They were nervous while waiting at Grand Central Station for Bryant and Rika. The kids were to spend the first three days of the Christmas vacation in New York and the remainder of the time of the holiday with the Guastellas. There were many doubts about Rika even though they had yet to meet her. A welcome had to be just the right touch, warm but not overwhelming, friendly and yet not over indulging. Somewhere between not quite accepting her and not giving the impression that they were rejecting her. Under the guise of protecting Bryant, the role as parents and their liberal philosophy were being put to the test.

Rika was apprehensive as the train entered the station. She so much wanted Bryant's parents to like her. If there was to be static from that direction it might be a complication in their otherwise smooth relationship. She could handle it, and she knew that Bryant would be supportive. His halo was as bright and imposing as ever. It would be much easier if it all went well. Her parents were crazy about Bryant. Imagine, they had allowed her to go with him on the overnight bus trip to Washington and now to New York for three days. They had complete confidence in him to care for their baby. Would the Yorks have the same trust in a cripple to look after their only son? At times, less frequently than before, her old disillusionment in people surfaced and tormented her. These were powerful forces to reckon with and difficult to subdue. She squeezed Bryant's hand and his smile was reassuring. His presence in her life did much to placate any demon that might threaten her.

Frieda's heart sagged as she saw Bryant supporting such a nondescript girl down the platform, a cane holding her up on the other side. The crowd had already rushed past them as they slowly made their way to the gate. She bit her lip, valiantly holding back the tears that swelled in her eyes. To want so much, to want the best for your child, and here he was guiding a person evidently not worthy of his affection and attention. Devotion needs to be earned and not given as a gift. This was going to be even more difficult than she had planned for. She grasped Carl's arm and saw the grimace on his face.

The initial meeting was awkward. The noise of the crowd, the train traffic and the pressing need to get to the subway to the apartment all contributed to an unsettled feeling and curtailed any conversation. Carl grabbed the small valise but Bryant insisted on carrying it even while holding on to Rika. Bryant knew his parents well and sensed they were initially disappointed. Hoping that events would not lead to choices, deeper breaths imparted the need for extra patience. Rika would not move from his side and as he glanced over at her small face he noted even through the glasses a stillness in her eyes that he had not seen before. It was that instant that he realized how much he had changed in this relatively brief period of time. It also made him aware that he felt her pain just as he felt her happiness. It brought a new appreciation for what they had together.

At the apartment, everyone seemed to relax. It was comforting to be in a quiet place after all of that commotion. As Bryant showed Rika his room they kissed, a long and emphatic kiss. Without speaking they just held each other. Just the thought that any situation was best handled together was reassuring.

Carl and Frieda started to get the meal together in the kitchen. Knowing looks said more than the words uttered. Frieda spoke first, her voice mimicking a faint whisper, "I am at a loss of what to do or what to say."

Carl's hushed response was unwavering, "We'll just pretend she is merely a friend of his and the situation is not as serious as we fear. What more can we do? It is not a question of gaining a daughter but losing a son. Time will bring him to his senses, I am sure. This is the first girl to pay him apt attention. There will be others. Hopefully, many others. The less serious we pretend it is may cast that spell on it."

"I hope you are right. I just feel so helpless. I keep thinking there should be something else we can do, some poignant words to utter. I think we are at the mercy of the situation and that lack of control threatens my very being."

Carl patted her arm. "It will turn out alright. We have no other choice but to think that way. After the milk is shaken the cream will settle to the top."

They all sat in the living room awaiting the roast to cook. There was cheese and crackers and apple cider. Rika started to feel more comfortable, more relaxed. After all, this was Bryant's family and it would be hers too. She started talking, perhaps more than she should. The gist of her dialogue was the admiration for the Yorks and the wonderful job they had done to raise such an intelligent, sensitive, and wonderful son. She could not keep her eyes off of Bryant, and everything she said was the truth as she saw it, as she felt it. Just when she was sure that she could not love him any stronger, an impulse carried her to a further magnificent level. Since his parents were an extension of him, the love engulfed them as well. So, she spoke freely, and her animated conversation sparked reaction and input from the entire gathering.

The facile and interesting conversation carried through the meal and well into the evening. Frieda was the first to succumb to Rika's charm and wit. The disabled body faded into the background supplanted by a sharp and engaging mind enhanced by varied facial expressions. What emerged in Frieda's mind was a captivating personality that held her spellbound. The obvious strong love that Rika felt for Bryant prompted an ease in Frieda identifying with her as a woman. It would be most difficult for a mother not to feel empathy for a woman who so completely worshipped her son.

Carl reluctantly became entranced by Rika and gradually fell under her warm and imposing charm. He studied the facial expressions, measured the words and concepts and eventually saw in Rika a composite of many of his favorite and most promising students. In spite of her lack of beauty, an awkward absence of female grace, there was an allure of her entire being that obliterated any outward weakness or imperfection. The one gnawing thought that kept emerging was that it was a pity that he and Frieda never had a daughter.

Bryant basked in the glow as he discerned his parents warming up to Rika. At least this hurdle had been surmounted. At this juncture it was so important that his parents become fond of her. In his mind there was no doubt that his own future included her and might even revolve around her. Her presence had brought out the Bryant he was meant to be, the Bryant he wanted to be. Her being at his side was destined to be a constant, an absolute.

The Yorks did not react in any prudish fashion when Bryant led Rika to his room for the night. The sleeping arrangements had not been discussed. It was accepted as it turned out to be.

Later, as the elder Yorks lay in their bed they digested the day's turn of events. "We have once again been proven wrong," Frieda whispered.

Carl patted her arm. "Yes, in a way. I am glad about it too."

"So am I. She is captivating in such a wholesome way. I can hug her tightly each time she looks at Bryant with so much love in her eyes. It must come from the heart, deep in the heart."

"Captivating is a good way to describe it. I think our preparation for confrontation has melted into total acceptance."

"Funny how life repeatedly teaches us such lessons."

23

Final exams proved to be a strenuous time for all. Socialization was kept at a minimum while full out studying took precedence. Bryant and Phil studied together, and it helped to keep them focused. Both received high grades. That brought a great sigh of relief. Rika's steady mind led her to the usual high achievement.

Nothing more was said officially from the University about the articles which did not let up on the forceful tone and message even just carrying Rika's name as the writer. Unfortunately, the impact did not seem to be as effective as hoped for. While student reaction was positive and growing, there was no budging any type of official action away from the impending fighting. The Vietnam situation was growing more serious. Young men were fleeing to Canada to avoid the draft. Demonstrations were becoming more frequent and garnering larger numbers of protestors. There was a great division in the nation, and the chasm was becoming wider and deeper.

Events affecting them on a personal level came as a bolt out of the blue. Student deferments were abolished. The only deferment other than for medical reasons was for married men. Since Bryant was at the priority age for call-up, Rika suggested that they marry. After all, they were deeply in love and totally committed to one another. It was a logical decision with the urgency only prompted by circumstances. They discussed the possibilities and decided that they should include their parents in the plan. Rika was sure her parents would go along with it and insist on a church wedding. Bryant hoped for a similar positive attitude from his folks. If there was any opposition, they would elope.

After dinner, Rika brought it up as the family still sat around the table. She cleared her throat and spoke with a firmness to convey the finality of the decision. "I have something to tell you all. It will not shock you, I hope, but its timing might surprise you. Before you say anything, please hear me out. Bryant and I are planning to get married. We are in love and convinced we are right for each other. In a more perfect world we probably would have waited until we were out of school. The world is now far from perfect and compels certain decisions. By marrying now it will ensure that Bryant will not be drafted. He will not have to participate in a war we do not believe in. I will not have to worry each day that he might be taken away from me and maybe even killed. I could not face a life without him. I love you all. Please do not oppose me on this. There is no other way. Think of it merely as the hastening of what was inevitable."

There was no gushing voice of shock or reproach. Each family member looked around the table into the faces of the group, letting the news sink in and gathering words to say that would be reasonable and convincing.

Jean thought to herself that this was a moment she never thought would arrive for her little girl. How could she deny her chance at love and happiness? She worshipped Bryant for who he was and what he had done for Rika.

Salvo wanted only the best for his darling little girl. In many ways he had already considered Bryant as a son and respected him for his ambition and ability. Marriage would not be an easy road for them but he was all in favor of them having the chance to succeed at it. After all, he and Jean had started out with little but themselves when they married.

Tess was inwardly torn. If only she could have the good fortune to feel what Rika was feeling. If only she could have the chance at happiness that Rika was approaching. She cared for Phil but was not sure there would be more than that. Whatever life had in store for her she would not and could not deny Rika her happiness.

Jean began to cry. Salvo rushed to her side to comfort her. "These are not sad tears," she said between sobs. "I am overjoyed for my precious daughter."

Salvo looked quickly over at Tess and accepted her nod. "Dearest Rika, we are surprised but pleasantly so. We only want what is best for you, only want you to be happy. I speak for us all. We totally understand your decision and you have our blessing."

Tess moved to Rika and hugged her firmly. "I should have been the first to marry. I relinquish that privilege to you, my dear sister. My heart is full for you as it always will be."

"Thank you all, my wonderful family. I have reached a new plateau in my life where I can see so many things clearly. One of those is the importance of family. Without your nourishment over the years I would not have grown to the point where I could recognize a chance for my own happiness and success and then to be bold enough to grab it and hold on to it. With your support now, it will further enable me to sustain that opportunity and to build my own family. You will always be a part of that. Bryant has grown to love you. This is not a separation of a family. It is an extension of its formidable power." Hugs all around sealed the approval and solidified the prospect.

The Yorks had anticipated just such a move. In fact, they were close to suggesting it themselves. Anything to keep Bryant out of the fighting forces. Rika had so won them over they did not flinch when Bryant announced the plan. Frieda had an inward reservation. Matters were never set in cement and any marriage could succumb to changes. It had not been feasible for her. For Bryant it would be different if it came to pass.

24

Three weeks later they were married. To placate Rika's parents it was a small church wedding attended only by the immediate family. Relatives balked at not being included but it was not the right time for a big celebration. Phil was the best man, and Tess was the maid of honor. Salvo was beaming from ear-to-ear as he made the way down the aisle with Rika on his arm. Her cane was in reality supporting both of them.

Rika looked and felt radiant. It was a special moment in any girl's life. For a handicapped person who never thought her life would take on normal proportions, it had additional significance. She had arrived at a place where a few brief months ago she thought she would never see or know. The in-depth experience and passion of a complete love was ample compensation for her incomplete body. She cherished every feeling, every emotion that made her a total woman. There was no denying that she was a full and contented human being. The receiving and giving of love were equally fulfilling. It was one motion, one ideal. Both were glorious in their own right, and quite magnificent in the combination. Her mate was her partner in mind and spirit. Both were dedicated to help people, to pursue unpopular causes if necessary, and to strive towards making a world more hospitable and caring.

Bryant put his arm around Rika's waist right after the ceremony. He kissed her cheek just below her glasses, making it as tender a kiss as possible. He was still immersed in the belief of symbolism. The tenderness was the reflection of his huge feelings for her and their life together. He had come to Blantyre as a shy boy. Upon his founding of love and the purpose of a potential endeavor that might allow him to penetrate the injustice and inequality that permeated so many aspects of society, he felt as a man. A conviction and a plan to carry it forward are stepping-stones to growth. He would be no ordinary man but one who could observe with discretion, act with purposeful design, and succeed with a robust desire to accomplish all that could be done.

It was silent in the church as the ceremony ended. Before they set out for a wedding dinner at Luigi's, with Luigi kindly closing the restaurant to all but the wedding party, each person looked on at Bryant's loving gesture towards Rika. Their feelings and thoughts had a chance to take shape and expression, even though it was just to themselves.

Jean looked upon the loving couple and her heart was full. In the few weeks preparing for the wedding it became so clear that the blessed turn of events for Rika had actually allowed her to come to terms with her own life. Feeling guilty for Rika's incapacity, she had transferred the loneliness and exclusion from a normal life that she was sure that Rika would suffer through to herself. Upon Rika's finding of love it released Jean from this self-imposed bondage. The romance and passion she had so coveted for herself was in reality the wish she had for Rika. Inwardly believing that it was an impossibility, that became her penance. Jean was now mercifully freed from this great guilt. Lifted from her shoulders was this great weight of her imaginary burden. The wedding completed her catharsis.

Salvo was filled with pride and hope. Always believing that Rika was special, here was the fruit of his faithful harvest. The years at a dull job that he endured just so he could be close to home and help as much as possible, and the years of an empty marriage, now seemed like a small price to pay for this moment. He had existed on sheer habit as each day and each motion was predictable. Now, Jean had miraculously turned to him with a new display of appreciation of him and with a positive attitude that the remaining years for them would be totally theirs. She now looked at him, listened to him, and there was a glisten in her eye of daring. He had never dreamed of such an eventuality.

Tess took many deep breaths during and after the wedding ceremony. Each breath brought a new resolve to turn her life around. Seeing and sensing the surge of happiness around her colored her outlook. She would try to find a job and strive to be successful at it. It was long overdue that she put the hurt and disappointment of her past behind her. Being so close to Rika's awakening filled her with hope for herself. She doubted that there would be any romantic conclusion from the friendship with Phil. Yet, he had shown her that there are gentle and considerate people in the world that can be worthy of her trust. She would be thankful for that and would be his friend to the extent he needed one.

Frieda clenched Carl's hand. Before her was her only child who had just declared his vows to another woman. She thought she might be jealous or upset but she found herself at ease with the situation and with herself. She envied Rika in finding such a fulfilling romance, a prospect that was unlikely for her. Reduced to dreams, she would carry on attempting to hold fast to the limited life she had. As a strong woman, the call upon that strength was just now becoming apparent.

Carl was sure that events had moved too fast for him to comprehend all of the components. Being a teacher for so many years he was accustomed to controlling people and situations. All that was transpiring was beyond his control. There was a firm pride in his son for the maturity and ambition he displayed. In spite of an inclination to dislike Rika and to discourage any romance, he had been completely charmed by her wholesome and natural personality. Not an easy victory for her, and it was that much more to her credit. He promised himself that he would be more attentive to Frieda. Taking her for granted for such a long time, he marveled at her bearing through the years. He earnestly believed that it was not too late for him to make up to her for his weaknesses.

Phil had ample opportunity in his position as best man to exude his newly acquired confidence. The happy event bolstered his determination to let the serious side of his character dominate over the jokester. He would show his father that the faith he had in him was not misplaced. He would assist Tess in overcoming her fear to let herself partake in life.

After the filling and boisterous dinner at Luigi's, Bryant and Rika returned to the basement of the Guastella house. A quick alteration had adequately prepared that domain for the couple to live somewhat of a private life for as long as they needed to. In each other's arms, they counted themselves as the real lucky people in this world. They had found this vital love, their families had become supportive and understanding, and all of the future battles would be fought together as shared views gave them the strength of unison. There would be turmoil and the quiet moments. The composite of their future, not yet fully determined, would be challenging. Their shadow selves might extend far before them and far behind them. For their being there would be no ending. Love would see to that. Each action and every phase would be just a beginning.